A Quiet Service

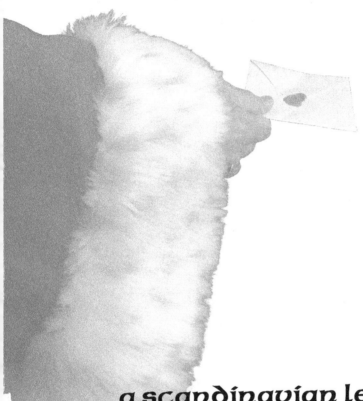

a scandinavian legacy

E. Gale Buck

The Silver Wreath
Keeping the True Magic of
Christmas Alive in Everyday

All rights reserved. No part of this book shall be reproduced or transmitted in any form or by any means, electronic, mechanical, magnetic, photographic including photocopying, recording or by any information storage and retrieval system, without prior written permission of the publisher. No patent liability is assumed with respect to the use of the information contained herein. Although every precaution has been taken in the preparation of this book, the publisher and author assume no responsibility for errors or omissions. Neither is any liability assumed for damages resulting from the use of the information contained herein.

Copyright © 2020 by The Silver Wreath
E. Gale Buck, Author

ISBN: 978-1-7321681-3-8 (paperback)

This is a work of Literary Fiction encompassing Small Town and Rural fiction, Adventure, and Holidays
    Historical Fiction; Christmas; Santa Claus; Saint Nicholas
    Suitable for Young Adult - Adult

Image on back cover by K. C. Ramsay

Published May 2020 by
The Silver Wreath
Raleigh NC USA
www.woodsmanstories.com
www.santaswoodsman.com

Printed in United States of America
by Ingram Lightning Source

Table of Contents

The Lineage of Santa's Woodsmen 1

The Legend of Santa's Woodsman 3

Introduction 5

I Jonathon Syzmoor 7

II Andrew Grieg 17

III Abram Grieg 67

    Nathaniel's Stars 88

The Grieg Family Legacy
    A Family in Devoted Service 95

IV Jameson Thorpe 99

Other books by author E Gale Buck 153

Dedication

This work is dedicated to all who read its pages searching for answers to their own problems and to those who seek to continue to believe in the True Magic of Christmas. This "Magic" is available to all who reach out and help another with their problems. May you all find something of yourself within the lives of *Santa's Woodsmen*.

Thank You

Saint Nicholas flies his wondrous sleigh on Christmas Morning, yet requests for all sorts of help come to him throughout the year. Just as Nicholas needs help with these requests, writers need help refining and completing their efforts. No literary work is ever done by just one person. I would like to thank all the Santas I have come to know and work with, for their influence and help developing these stories. I would also like to thank the writers - Drew, Leslie, Lauren, Robin, and Michael - who have helped me grow in my ability to tell a story by allowing me to read their work and creatively critiquing my own. Those wonderful people who have read this work, sometimes multiple times, and have helped me refine the complex stories of *Santa's Woodsmen* - it isn't all just translating diaries. And most of all my Bride, Christmasana, who has read these tales almost as many times as I have, spent countless hours editing and "counseling" me on verbiage, as well as living the lives of these incredible men and women through my writing and discoveries about each. Serving the requests of Nicholas is a "family affair." To each of you I owe my gratitude and humble thanks.

The Lineage of Santa's Woodsmen

Jonathon Syzmoor began an unusual relationship with Nicholas, a man better known as Santa Claus. Since that time the title, responsibilities, and honor of being *Santa's Woodsman* has been passed down through family lines, across to friends and associates, and down even more family lines. While quietly working in service to Saint Nicholas, each Woodsman has found a new piece of Nicholas' complex existence and personality. These are the men and women who have served with the man in the red cape.

Woodsman's Name	Years of Service
a scandinavian legacy	
1. Jonathon Syzmoor	1831 - 1850
2. Andrew Grieg, grandson of Jonathon	1844 - 1891
3. Abram Grieg, son of Andrew	1866 - 1890
4. Jameson Thorpe, recruited	1890 - unknown
exploring a new world	
5. Artur "Arthur" Thorpe, son of Jameson	1922 - 1932
passion beyond misfortune	
6. Maxwell Kartar, acquaintance of Arthur	1932 - 1932
7. Edith Kartar, wife of Maxwell	1932 - 1943
8. James "Jimmy" Norfleet, friend	1943 - 1961
9. Bethany Norfleet, daughter of "Jimmy"	1960 - 1972
reaching beyond tomorrow	
10. Charles Longfellow, recruited	1972 - 1973
11. Michael Tompkins, recruited by Charles	1973 - 1992
12. Kristopher Fordham, cousin to Michael	1992 - 2007
13. Gale Buck, recruited by Kristopher	2007 - Present

Note: throughout these records you will find the name "Alapouella Pohjantähti" which is the proper name of the village at the North Pole. The correct pronunciation of this name is alaPOella pozanTAtee, or simply "A.P."

The Legend of Santa's Woodsman

Jonathon Syzmoor met Nicholas in the middle of a forest on a star-filled, cold winter night as Jonathon was delivering food to families in need. Since that time those fortunate enough to inherit the title of *Woodsman* have served the requests of Nicholas according to their own talents and abilities. Some delivered food, wood, and supplies; some did special jobs in the community; some changed the course of history to the improvement of their fellow citizens of the world. All have enjoyed the special company of the gentleman in the red cape and all have served his requests as best they could.

Through relationships with Nicholas, the man in the red cape, *The Woodsmen* have come to know many of the secrets of this wonderful man who is surrounded by enigmatic mystery. These tales, and the truths behind the legends of the "red suit" have been handed down from one generation of *Woodsman* to the next, and expanded by each servant's personal experiences.

One of the more delightful aspects of my service as *The Woodsman* is relating stories of the mysterious man in the red suit. Indeed Nicholas laughs with delight when he hears of his stories being told to people who might have lost their belief in his reality.

You may have never heard of *Santa's Woodsman* and this is no surprise, for *The Woodsman* has always sought to be anonymous, never seeking credit nor recognition for his / her deeds. However, my task as current *Woodsman* has brought this servant out of the shadows, for my task is to restore belief in the man in the red cape / suit and all that he represents. *The Woodsman* has truly become *Santa's Woodsman*.

As you journey through the lives of the thirteen Woodsmen, do not be surprised if you find something personal, a tug at your own heart, a reflection of yourself. For while the commission of *The Woodsman* or *Santa's Woodsman* may belong to only a few, men and women who live ordinary lives made extraordinary through love and service, their journeys and Nicholas' magic belong to each of us.

A Quiet Service — *a scandinavian legacy*

Introduction

I became the Thirteenth *Woodsman* of Saint Nicholas at 10:28 a.m. on the eighth of November 2007. What little I had learned of this impressive lineage to this point told me first that I was in a special group and second, I did not belong here. Still, I agreed to serve, even though I had no idea how I was to serve. (Not uncommon among new Woodsmen.) Previous *Woodsmen* had been successful men and women who took action without hesitation. People who saw possibilities in almost every situation. I am an author and storyteller, a "man of Christmas," yet reluctant to wear the red suit of "Santa Claus." What could I do?

The solution to my conundrum arrived three days later, at 1:27 Monday morning. I woke from a fast sleep, fully alert to a sensation of something needing to be taken care of. It took me several minutes to waken enough to collect my thoughts. Following pure impulse, I went to our back door where I found three medium-sized boxes stacked in our carport. An attached note read, "Tell their stories to the world." Inside were logs, journals, and diaries of twelve preceding *Woodsmen*, with notes from Nicholas. I carried these boxes to our living room, locked the door, and went back to bed. This had to be a dream.

My first attempt at sharing the story of "Santa's Woodsmen" was to tell how this tradition of service began. *The Woodsman's Tale - share your life without expectation*, was first published in October 2010. I then struggled with secrets I learned from these wondrous journals, publishing *Finding Nicholas - secrets of santa revealed by his woodsmen* one year later, November 2011. My charge, however, was to "tell their stories to the world." *Their stories*, these men and women, individuals, who quietly accepted Nicholas' call, providing help to those in need, as his *Woodsmen*. Each led a normal life, just like you and me. These were ordinary people who answered an extraordinary call, to help people find the True Spirit of Christmas year round. They shared their lives without expectation.

When the story of these remarkable people was completed, *A Quiet Service - the lineage of santa's woodsmen*, reviewers suggested this journey would be better divided into four volumes.

A Quiet Service - a scandinavian legacy
A Quiet Service - exploring a new world
A Quiet Service - passion beyond misfortune
A Quiet Service - reaching beyond tomorrow

A Quiet Service - a scandinavian legacy starts at the beginning of the lineage, with Jonathon Syzmoor, in Katril, Sweeden. Our legend continues with Jonathon's grandson, Andrew Grieg, who was responsible for the birth of *The Woodsman* tradition. Andrew's son completes the Grieg Legacy, however the lineage continues in Namsskogan, Norway with Jameson Thorpe. Each of these men shared their lives without expectation, but not always without question.

I
Jonathon Syzmoor
1831 - 1850
Born 1788, Katril, Sweden
Died 1850, Katril, Sweden

Jonathon's story comes from his own log books, the diaries of his family and the memories of Nicholas.

Introduction

By age forty-three Jonathon Syzmoor had been orphaned by the deaths of both parents, learned more than a trade, and built an empire. He lost the most important person in his life almost as quickly as he found her, rejected his only daughter, and was shamed by his four-year-old grandson for not doing what needed to be done. Awakened by regret for what he had not done, Jonathon sought to repair his past by enlisting the aid of his sister who could inform him of those within his local community who needed special help. Because he always left a bundle of firewood when he made his secret visits, this anonymous spirit of generosity and aid became known as *The Woodsman*.

Jonathon's Story

When Jonathon was only eight years old, his father was killed in a logging accident. Two years later his mother, sick with influenza, and his younger brother both died when their cottage caught fire. His sister suffered severe burns in this same fire. Needing to find a way to get his sister out of their poverty, Jonathon left home to find a skill. He returned six years later to find his village in despair, beaten down under rules enacted by the man who now controlled industry in their county, Arthur Westmend. Believing the best way to relieve suffering of his community was to work with the source of the problems, Jonathon secured a business arrangement with

Mister Westmend. During the next year this unusual young man made numerous shrewd and profitable transactions, emerging very wealthy and in control of The Westmend Innehav[1], the legal holdings of Arthur Westmend, which impacted several counties in north central Sweden.

Arthur Westmend became Jonathon's partner as well as his father-in-law, for Jonathon also fell in love with Westmend's daughter, Kathryn. The two men journeyed together often, exploring land acquisitions, business opportunities, and meeting with clients of their lumber and other industries.

Jonathon made many changes for the well being of his county, however it was his wife, Kathryn, who was more important to him than life itself. Theirs was a life of splendor and accomplishment. One of Jonathon's favorite pastimes was spending evenings with Kathryn behind their manor, exploring the stars and planning new adventures for tomorrow. Jonathon nearly raptured with delight when he learned that he and Kathryn would soon be parents.

When Kathryn was in her eighth month, Jonathon and Arthur went to explore an estate they sought to acquire. Their visit was cut short by an outbreak of influenza in this region. Weeks later Arthur became extremely ill. As Kathryn's time to deliver the baby came nearer she too became ill.

Kathryn's baby was taken from her moments before she succumbed to the fatal disease. Arthur died at the same moment as his daughter. Jonathon was sitting with the lifeless body of Arthur when the doctor told him of the birth of his daughter and the death of his wife.

Suddenly losing everyone he held dear, Jonathon threw himself into his business, leaving his sister, Rebecca, to raise his daughter, Sarah. As Sarah grew, her presence exposed painful memories for Jonathon about the loss of her mother. Unable to overcome his pain, Jonathon severed relationships with his daughter. Rebecca could not stand the resulting isolation within the manor house and took Sarah to live with her in Katril when she turned twelve years old.

---

[1] Innehav - legal holdings, whether or not in actual possession

Sarah eventually married a man who worked for Jonathon. Theirs was a happy and rewarding life raising three children and caring for others around their small village. She never saw her father. Shortly after her husband was killed in a logging accident, Sarah became extremely ill. Jonathon discovered her circumstance quite by accident. Overcome by Sarah's situation, he assumed full responsibility for his ailing daughter. Jonathon immediately moved his daughter and three grandchildren, who had never met him, into his manor. Finding his sister, who lived next to Sarah, near exhaustion, he moved Rebecca to his manor at this same time.

During their first dinner together, Andrew, the oldest of Sarah's three children woke Jonathon to the circumstance of many families in his counties of concern. Improvements he and his wife, Kathryn, had made years earlier for the welfare of the community had faded away without his attention. Just as when Arthur Westmend held the village in his grip, villagers worked long hours leaving little time to develop gardens or rest. Even clean water and firewood were scarce.

Realizing the devastation his neglect had wrought, Jonathon resolved to make amends to his daughter by continuing her legacy of caring. He began delivering food, wood, and clothing to families in need. Not wanting further ridicule for his neglect nor recognition for his efforts, these deliveries were made in secret, under cover of darkness. Every delivery included wood and a rebuilt fire, which led to the anonymous benefactor becoming known as "The Woodsman." Sarah died without ever gaining realization that she was being care for in her father's manor nor what he had undertaken.

On a star-filled, cold winter night the Woodsman had delivered food and supplies to the first of three intended homes in central Scandinavia. Jonathon had gone but a short distance toward the second cottage when he saw a man standing beside the road. This stranger was tall, had a long full beard, and wore a scarlet hooded cape which appeared to be trimmed with white fur. Without hesitation or fear Jonathon pulled his sleigh to a stop near the cloaked figure.

"Mr. Syzmoor, would you care for some companionship

this evening?" a quiet but strong voice called out.

Jonathon quickly looked around for signs of other men hiding in the forest. Was this an ambush? As Jonathon's attention returned to the mysterious figure he was drawn to the stranger's eyes. This man presented a quiet confidence and his gentle smile gave Jonathon a warming comfort. Jonathon's thoughts returned to his mission and fearing his secret would be revealed, he reluctantly responded, "Normally I would welcome companionship, however this evening I am on a mission of great importance. Is there something I could do for you?"

"I am aware of your visits. You have just left the cottage of the Rumbolt family. Now I believe you are on your way to Mistress Rumbolt's cousin, Sara Brandt, and then, if I am not mistaken, the home of Jon Vrought. Do not be alarmed for I arranged these visits through Rebecca. These names were given to your sister anonymously, of course. May I join you?"

Jonathon nodded and the man stepped into the sleigh as though it were an old friend. A quick whistle and click of the reins and the sleigh resumed its journey. Arriving at the next home, Jonathon picked up a side of meat and bundle of wood from the back of his sleigh. The visitor collected a bundle of blankets. Without a word between them, the two men divided duties and upon completing their tasks returned to the sleigh.

"How is your business doing?" Jonathon's guest asked as they began their journey to the third cottage. "I imagine you are feeling a bit overwhelmed right now."

Jonathon filled with apprehension once again, how could this stranger know about his business? Debating how he should answer, or whether to answer, Jonathon looked across at his unexpected companion. Something about his manner and his soft gaze relaxed The Woodsman. He confirmed that what the gentleman offered was correct.

The old man continued, "You need to be careful with your business. Should word get out about your midnight visits, you could be overcome by requests for assistance, many of them exaggerated. You are a wise businessman, however you may find it difficult to separate your business from your aid. You must maintain your business or your ability to offer aid will cease. Do you understand this?" His voice was soft, comforting, and compassionate.

"Yes, I do. I do not understand who you are, nor how you know so much about me?"

"I have been around for quite some time . . . visiting in the towns and villages. You have gained a reputation as being a hard but fair businessman . . . purely business. I learned that you were once very generous, until your wife died and you retreated into your sorrow.

"Sorrow is an important part of living. I read once that 'a life void of sorrow is a life not yet lived to its fullest potential.' Through sorrow you learn compassion, however yours has been somewhat extreme. Then I began to hear stories of a ghost called The Woodsman, emerging shortly after your daughter's death. I did not put you together with The Woodsman until recently when I saw you rescue men stranded in a snow storm."

Jonathon became defensive, replying firmly, "Those men were in my employ. It would have been foolish of me, and costly, to let anything happen to them."

Conversation ended as they arrived at the third cottage. As before, the two men silently divided their chores. Jonathon sliced meat and put some on a plate for the children, should they awaken before their parents. He then stacked wood and stoked the fire. The visitor spread out blankets and said a prayer over each of the sleeping family members. Returning to the sleigh, the guest asked if he might handle the reins. Feeling strangely at ease with this unusual situation, Jonathon smiled affirmation.

"You should know that this sleigh was designed to be pulled by caribou or reindeer. The leather tether fits their build much better and their shorter legs will not damage the front panel. Your horses are forcing a short stride so as not to hit the panel." Jonathon watched the horses and saw that the old man was correct. "Jonathon, you are indeed a good man with a good heart, but you need to establish a routine for your midnight rides. Trying to help everyone will tire your household and your body. Take care of your loved ones first, for they are your inspiration and the source of your strength in your personal life and professional ventures. Guard your business, it is a very large part of who you are. When you get your heart and your mind working together, your life will become like a fine timepiece." He pulled the reigns gently, bringing the sleigh to a stop. Silently, he removed a silver watch from his pocket. Opening the back cover he continued, "See how the parts of this timepiece interact in perfect harmony? You can only achieve this harmony if all parts are in balance with one another." He then looked into Jonathon's eyes and placed the watch into his hand.

Jonathon stared at this man with awe and confusion. When the sleigh resumed its journey Jonathon looked down at the watch, carefully pushing it safely into his pocket. As the sleigh continued to slide through the moonlit forest, only the sound of their horses pushing through the snow could be heard. After a time the old man pulled the sleigh to a stop once again and looked into Jonathon's face with a gentle intensity. "My friend, there are two more things you need to consider as you continue your journey. First, it is not your responsibility to save the world from poverty. Poverty and hunger are a sickness of humanity that have been around for all time. You did not cause them and while you can relieve some of the suffering they create, you cannot cure them. Second, as you share your life with others expect nothing in return. Many of your beneficiaries will take your gifts and continue as though you had never blessed them. Others will merely put their hands out for another gift; fortunately these are few. However a few will bless you for your giving and lift themselves, even sharing with others as they are able. You have no way of knowing what your gifts may bring from others, but your life will be far richer for sharing it. Enjoy!" The old man stepped from the sleigh and handed the reins to Jonathon. "Thank you for this evening. It has been a pleasure."

"Excuse me, but what is your name?" Jonathon called to his guest.

"I have been called by many names, but the name given to

me at birth is Nikolaos, or Nicholas to your tongue. Good night." The old man then climbed into a small sleigh that was waiting for him a short distance away. Two reindeer harnessed to the sleigh began to sprint through the shadows of the midnight forest. Little did Jonathon realize that this meeting was the beginning of a relationship that would span many generations and effect countless lives around the world.

~~~~~~~~~~~~~~~~~~~~~~~

Jonathon's nighttime identity was kept secret, for Nicholas' advice confirmed his own fears that should he be discovered many hands that could be helping themselves would be demanding his assistance. His household staff knew of his secret identity and deliveries for they assisted by preparing bundles of roast venison and pork, baskets of bread, cheese, potatoes, and occasionally fruit. His housekeeper procured blankets and clothing, and listened for information about families in need while at the market. Most requests for assistance from *The Woodsman* came from the local priest and Jonathon's sister. Neither knew the true identity of *The Woodsman*, believing him to be a friend of Jonathon.

Jonathon Syzmoor was meticulous with details in business. He never fashioned any contract that would not result in benefit for all parties involved. However, because he was so meticulous with details and familiar with each and every provision of his contracts, Jonathon acquired incredible wealth. One of his favorite acquisitions was an estate in the northern regions of Sweden, near Bradsvald. This estate included a mill for producing furniture grade lumber and a hunting lodge, which he used to house wood cutters and mill workers. While the lodge was a place to relax it also presented many opportunities for both Jonathon and *The Woodsman*.

Sarah Syzmoor Grieg was raised by Jonathon's sister Rebecca and never knew Jonathon as her father. Sarah's children, however, enjoyed the attention and goodness of their grandfather. Andrew, Angela, and Kathryn taught Jonathon how to be both father and grandfather. He learned his lessons well and never again shrank from these pleasures or responsibilities.

As *The Woodsman* was returning home late one evening, he happened upon the youngest granddaughter, Kathryn, and two other children of the Syzmoor household trying to catch Gnarlish, a local gnome of legend. He had but one delivery this night so he used Odin, his white reindeer to carry the parcels as he rode White Spirit, his white stallion. After hiding his companions, he removed his coat and tied its hood over his head so the coat flapped about as he moved. When he could see the children were at a safe distance and location, he began to dance about and sing in a "gnarlish" tongue. Then stopping his dance with his back to the children, he became very still. Summoning all his strength he leapt into the air and turned, landing on a boulder that had been behind him. Chanting a magical incantation, he waved both hands in the direction of the young nighttime adventurers.

All three children ran the entire distance back to the manor. Jonathon, however, had one more antic to polish off the evening. Quickly, he pulled his coat back on and mounted White Spirit. Releasing Odin, he lay low on Spirit's back and called loudly to both of them, "HOME, as fast as you can!" The children could not help but see the ghostly iridescent images of the stallion and reindeer that were said to haunt the woods of this region.

Becoming a grandfather led Jonathon to become *The Woodsman* and as *The Woodsman,* Jonathon learned lessons which afforded him opportunities to help others and his business. While riding through villages late at night, he would occasionally notice homes with lights on. He would then see if a cart or sleigh of doctor or priest was present. After making inquiries about the family of the house in question, Jonathon might offer the assistance of his vast holdings, The Syzmoor Innehav. He purchased mortgages in trouble, estates at below market values, and even hired men and families to manage properties they already lived on and once owned. The Syzmoor Innehav was large and successful because Jonathon found creative ways to help those who were in need and were deserving of special consideration, while preserving their pride and integrity.

Nicholas visited Jonathon frequently, not only bringing names of families in need of help, but also being a friend. This friendship strengthened *The Woodsman*, giving him courage and stamina to continue through demanding efforts to serve the needs of a growing community entrusted to his care.

Jonathon Syzmoor died at the age of 62 after serving his community to varying degrees for a lifetime and working with Nicholas as *The Woodsman* for nineteen wonder-filled years. Attendance at his funeral exceeded the capacity of the small chapel and the village square as well.

Editor's Note: the life of Jonathon Syzmoor is described briefly only to acquaint the reader with the origin of an uncommon relationship with Saint Nicholas and how this relationship became *The Woodsman* tradition. To fully appreciate the sacrifice and quiet service of Jonathon Syzmoor please read *The Woodsman's Tale - share your life without expectation*[2]

---

[2] *The Woodsman's Tale - share your life without expectation* by E. Gale Buck (c) 2010. Available in paperback and kindle format at www.amazon.com or www.thereindeerplace.com.

II
Andrew Grieg
1844 - 1891
Born 1826, Katril, Sweden
Died unknown

Andrew kept very few logs or letters as The Woodsman. Early parts of his story come from the logs of his grandfather, Jonathon Syzmoor. Later chapters are from the diaries of his wife and journals of his children. Nicholas provided his personal memories to complete Andrew's story.

Introduction

Andrew grew up with tales of the *Woodsman*, however it was a week before Mid-Winter in his nineteenth year before he actually met him. Dark falls early this time of year and he was arriving home late in the evening on Winter Break. Needing to discuss important news with his grandfather, he had spent most of the journey home preparing for this conversation. Andrew was mentally prepared, but as he rode into the manor courtyard his grandfather was stepping into a sleigh. Dressed in a white cloak, Jonathon had a white reindeer and small white stallion harnessed to his sleigh. Andrew's heart began to pound and he could barely breathe. His prepared speech, indeed all thoughts, flew from his mind.

"Okay, either get in the sleigh or go inside. But you will have to move for I have several deliveries to make." Jonathon held up his hands waiting for a decision. Not sure what to do, Andrew pushed his horse into a stall and jumped into the sleigh. "So how is school?" Jonathon asked in a simple straightforward tone.

"You are *The Woodsman*?!" Andrew exclaimed, filled with confusion and uncertainty. "You ARE *The Woodsman*!" he repeated realizing what was happening. He was leaving on a midnight journey in *The Woodsman's* sleigh with *The Woodsman*, his Grandfather!

Andrew's Story

Andrew Grieg, named for his father's father, was the first born son of Marc Grieg and Sarah Syzmoor. Born in Katril, Andrew grew up under the watchful eye of his mother's aunt Rebecca; no one in the village knew of his relationship to Jonathon Syzmoor. Andrew was in all regards a healthy and inquisitive boy. His favorite pastime involved moving things, such as his father's pipe, his mother's scissors or knitting needles, anything he could wrap his little hands around and pick up. He found great delight in picking up an object, carrying it around for a period of time, and putting it down when he tired of it - wherever he happened to be at the moment. Marc and Sarah's mantle became the safe place for all things moveable by Andrew.

Angela, Andrew's first sister, was born when Andrew was about a year and a half. Kathryn joined the family two years later. Aunt Rebecca watched over the family from her cottage, just a few yards away. Rebecca helped to raise the growing family as she had raised Sarah, in a warm caring community away from the cold indifference of the Syzmoor manor.

Marc and Sarah, Andrew's parents, were loved by the entire village, not just for their caring personalities but also for their generosity of spirit. They were always willing to do more than most to help anyone in need. Marc worked as a crew chief for The Syzmoor Innehav, his crew always exceeding their quota. Whenever managers tried to break up Marc's crew, saying they were needed elsewhere, not one of them would ever leave or accept promotion out of the village. The crew enjoyed working with Marc.

When Andrew was four years old, his father suffered serious injuries in an icy logging accident and had to be carried home on a stretcher. Returning from tending to a sick family, Rebecca encountered Marc's work crew. Instructing the men to take Marc to her cottage Rebecca went to get Sarah. Upon hearing the news, Sarah ran to her aunt's cottage without protection from the icy wet weather. She reached Marc as her aunt arrived at the door behind her; both of them were breathless. Sarah wiped the icy rain from Marc's face. The touch of her hand opened his eyes. Smiling softly he took her hand. Sarah breathed deeply when she felt his touch but did not realize he was unable to squeeze her hand. Their eyes locked and said more than any words could. Marc let out a slight breath and closed his eyes for the last time. Sarah did not shake him nor try to bring him back; she simply squeezed his hand and held it to her lips. Her eyes did not leave his face.

Jon, Marc's assistant, caught Rebecca as she collapsed. He called to Sarah several times before she replied. When Sarah saw that her aunt had collapsed and was pasty white, she let go of her husband's hand and began caring for Rebecca. Jon took three young Grieg children to his own cottage. Two days later Jonathon Syzmoor happened upon Sarah's cottage, finding both Sarah and Rebecca hovering near death. Jonathon collected the children and moved all to the manor house where his doctor could see to their care.

Chaos and confusion broke out when Jonathon arrived at the manor with two sick women and three unknown grandchildren. Andrew, being the oldest of the young children, quietly watched after his sisters. He looked at this strange man, who had snatched him from familiar surroundings, with wonder and suspicion as Jonathon began barking orders at him.

"Boy, your mother is very ill and her life could depend on you doing what I asked. Now, please, go quickly," Jonathon repeated his plea to Andrew.

Accepting that his mother needed help, Andrew ran to the front door as asked and called to Jon and Eric, who worked for Jonathon. Throughout the chaotic events young Andrew watched with curiosity and detachment. He stopped Missus Beorne, the manor cook, from giving Kathryn chocolate and made certain both sisters got enough to eat.

Rebecca recovered quickly and prepared to officiate at the first dinner with Jonathon and his three grandchildren. Jonathon entered the dining room after all others had arrived. Taking a deep breath, he addressed his butler and other staff, "Thank you, Jacob. Now, as the table is well-stocked, you may all go enjoy your dinner as well." Jonathon then seated Rebecca and assisted Andrew and Angela into their seats. Kathryn was already seated in a child's high chair. Jonathon introduced himself as he sat, "Children, I know you have not heard of me, but I am Jonathon Syzmoor. I am your mother's father."

Each of the three children looked at Jonathon with suspicion, their eyes showing confusion and distrust. Dinner proceeded with difficulties for everyone because they were all strangers. Only Rebecca knew the children and their grandfather. Conversation was limited. Rebecca, who had helped to raise the three children, assisted them in talking with Jonathon, who conducted himself as though he were at a business dinner with associates. At one point Jonathon looked up from cutting his meat and saw both Angela and Andrew pushing bits of bread and meat into their napkins.

Jonathon called to Andrew and Angela in a typical business manner, "Children, why are you putting food in your napkins?"

Both children grew wide-eyed and silent. Jonathon repeated his question.

"There is so much food here," Andrew began very sheepishly, "you have so much food and Kristian and Edvar have almost nothing on their table. I was going to take them some food when we go back to their house."

Jonathon was struck by the comment and looked to Rebecca for an explanation. "They speak of the Metzer family. Jon Metzer is, or was, Marc's assistant crew chief. He and his wife have five children and, like most of the village, have very little food to eat this time of year." They finished dinner in silence; Jonathon pushed remaining bits of food around his plate without taking a bite.

At that precise moment in time, four-year-old Andrew Grieg changed the course of history. Through his actions and words he erased the very self-centered Jonathon Syzmoor and awoke the man, his grandfather, who would become *The Woodsman*.

The two older children slept together for several days on a mattress laid on the floor until beds and child-size furniture arrived; Kathryn slept in a large laundry basket. Jacob did his best to help other men assemble the beds, but he was somewhat clumsy and slowed their progress. Once everything was assembled, Jacob did show the men who brought the furniture where to put it. Rebecca helped with arrangements as well.

Rebecca went back and forth between the children and Sarah, taking care of whomever needed her most at any given moment. Andrew and the girls would sit for hours holding their mother's hands as she slept. Occasionally she would waken, but these periods were brief and she would drift back to sleep without saying anything to anyone. Sarah's nurse tried to keep the children away. Jonathon kept bringing them back.

Jonathon spent a lot of time with his daughter, talking to her and holding her hand. He made a priority of checking on her before he would leave the manor and then again as soon as he returned, whether hours, days or even weeks later. Returning from a long trip to the northern region, Jonathon found the doctor in Sarah's room. "What is happening?" Jonathon asked, his voice shaking.

"She appears to be surrendering," the doctor replied.

Everyone came to Sarah's room and she opened her eyes. First she looked at her father and stared at him as though she were looking into his heart. She then looked to each person in the room, one by one. Once she had seen everyone in the room, she closed her eyes for the last time.

After another extended trip to the northern region, Jonathon invited the children into his study. Andrew watched patiently as Jonathon routinely pulled papers out of his satchel. Then Grandfather took out a small, soft doll and handed it to Kathryn. The youngest of the three grandchildren looked at it briefly, then held it close to her heart. The grandfather took out another doll, a bit larger than the first, with porcelain hands and head. He handed this doll to Angela. She smiled at Grandfather and he smiled back at her.

"I hope you don't have a doll in there for me," Andrew grumbled.

"No, young sir, for you I have a symbol of strength, endurance, and independence. One of nature's most beautiful animals." Grandfather then presented Andrew with a carved caribou. Andrew was speechless and studied the animal with growing interest. His fingers ran down the back, examining the smoothness. He seemed to absorb every detail of the carving as he made it a part of himself.

Several days later Andrew was unusually quiet at supper, until he suddenly looked straight at Jonathon and asked, "Grandfather, have you ever seen a caribou up close?"

Everyone quietly waited for an answer. "Yes, Andrew, I have. I was hunting at the lodge just last week and came across a small herd. I was going to shoot one for dinner, but they were so peaceful and beautiful. Besides, they were awfully small and didn't seem to offer much meat for a barn full of hungry men."

"Can you take me to see them, please?" Andrew looked intently at his grandfather.

"Suppose we all go to the lodge this spring, after the snow melts. While we are there, we can see about finding a herd of caribou."

Andrew thought for a few seconds and then nodded with a smile. "Yes, sir, that would be nice." Immediately, the table began to buzz about going to the lodge.

Weeks later, shortly before midwinter, conversation around the supper table was focused on the family. Jonathon asked Andrew if he would be interested in visiting the lodge in the coming weeks. Andrew hesitated until his grandfather added that he had seen caribou around the lodge. Beaming with delight, Andrew nodded excitedly.

Weeks later Jonathon, the three children, and their nanny left on a journey to the north. As their sleigh approached the lodge, Jonathon heard a loud commotion and shouting. Hors, the caretaker, and his entire family greeted him. All that is except Peder, who was admiring Jonathon's white stallion. Hors laughed almost uncontrollably as he greeted Jonathon. "My son, Peder, was checking on the animals in the stable when he saw your white stallion through the forest. He screamed that a spirit from heaven was coming to take him away. I am most glad that it was only one of His servants, and a most welcome one at that."

Once inside, Hors introduced his family: Hannah his wife, Kristina their youngest daughter and the same age as Andrew, Elen their oldest daughter, age eight, and Peder, age seven. Jonathon introduced Andrew, age four, Angela, age two, and Ingrid, their nanny.

"Mister Syzmoor, we are delighted to see you here in your lodge, but what brings you such a distance at midwinter?" Hors asked.

"There are several business matters which I need to ask you about regarding the mill, and my grandson seems to be very interested in caribou. Do you know if there is a herd nearby?"

"So, Mister Andrew, you are interested in caribou? Do you want one to pull your sleigh or to put on your plate?" Andrew looked at the strange man with the deep voice but did not answer. "Come here, son; I will show you some caribou." Hors put his hand out and after getting a nod of approval from Grandfather, Andrew went with him. Everyone followed closely as they went out the door and around the stable to the furthest corner of the lodge. "Look . . . caribou. They came in three or four days ago and have not left. The meat you will eat tonight is from another herd we found four, maybe five, kilometers from here. I come home from hunting and I have caribou at my own back door." Hors chuckled at his unnecessary effort.

While Jonathon and Hors talked about the caribou that had taken up residence and other game in the area, Andrew let go of Hors and walked toward the herd. He was within ten feet when he was noticed by Ingrid and Jonathon. Ingrid began to chase after him, but Jonathon stopped her.

Without concern for safety nor fear from any side, Andrew walked past the closest caribou and began stroking the second, a bull. The bull nuzzled Andrew's stomach knocking him into the snow. Andrew began to laugh uncontrollably, the bull pushing at his arms and legs. Several of the caribou did not like the laughter and started to leave, but the bull stood and with a single snort stopped their movement. Andrew stopped laughing and stood up. The caribou's head was too high for him to reach now, but the bull bent down and gently pushed Andrew toward people watching in amazement. Andrew stroked the bull's nose and returned to his grandfather.

Jonathon stood staring at the caribou in amazement. Hors asked Jonathon a question, but Jonathon did not hear for he was approaching the caribou. When he was about twelve feet from the closest animal, all disappeared into the darkened woods. Hors laughed at his attempt, "You did well; most people cannot come within twenty feet of a wild caribou. But your grandson has magic in his heart, I think."

Andrew's magic took hold again the following spring, when Jonathon and Andrew joined Gunther Hansen collecting caribou calves to build a new herd. Jonathon had hired Gunther to manage game on his northern holdings, but there was very little time available to safely capture young caribou. Andrew walked boldly into a wild herd and touched a two-day-old calf, which followed Andrew out of the herd where Gunther slipped a rope around its neck. Andrew repeated this technique until he had collected eight animals. Jonathon used a more traditional method of grab and carry, but managed to capture only one calf.

Hor's daughter, Kristina, was suspicious, as well as a bit jealous, of Andrew's gift. She had no desire to play with the caribou but could not understand why the animals would let Andrew walk up to them when no one else could. Kristina became rather fond of Andrew after he took her up to a wild caribou and the animal allowed her to stroke its head. At that moment a special friendship blossomed between these two young people.

One night when Andrew was about eight years old he awoke shortly after falling asleep, wanting a drink of water. Supper had been a bit spicy and his young mouth was dry. He rolled his tongue around for a minute listening to the quiet of the manor house before deciding to go down to the kitchen for some water. As he reached the top of the steps, Andrew saw a cloaked figure leaving through the front door. Curious about the late night visitor, Andrew hurried down the stairs to the dining room where a window looked out into the courtyard.

Light from a quarter moon shone dimly but stars shimmered brightly. Andrew briefly forgot about the visitor as he became mesmerized by the twinkling stars. Suddenly a low-riding sleigh pulled by a small white horse and a white reindeer passed through the middle of the courtyard, disappearing into the night.

"The Woodsman's sleigh," Andrew thought out loud. "Why would *The Woodsman* be visiting our house?" He puzzled for several seconds until the dryness of his mouth reminded him why he was out of bed. Continuing to the kitchen he poured a glass of water from a pitcher left on the table and thought as he drank, "Maybe he came to visit Grandfather."

After one last gulp of water, Andrew ran to his grandfather's study. It was empty and dark except for a few glowing embers in the fireplace. Looking around at shadows cast by the embers, Andrew found a single glass with an aroma of brandy still lingering. Yawning, he looked around the study once more before stumbling back to his bed.

Andrew went to the lodge in Bradsvald whenever his grandfather could arrange it. At first his interest was in helping Gunther Hansen raise reindeer, but as Andrew grew his interests expanded to include Kristina. When he was fifteen years old, he noticed Kristina had become a young lady. Fortunately for Andrew, she noticed that he was becoming a young man as well.

It happened quite by accident during one of their usual outings. Gunther was touring the estate with Jonathon, which left Andrew at the lodge with his sisters and Kristina. The girls organized an outing and conscripted Andrew to do the "carrying" for them. Peder left his own chores to help Andrew load three baskets of food and two blankets into the wagon and then get a team of horses harnessed. As the girls arrived for their outing, Peder quickly disappeared, returning to his abandoned work.

"Where shall we go?" Andrew asked his sisters and Kristina after all had climbed into the wagon.

"I would like an open field with a view," Kathryn replied.

"No, I prefer the shade of the trees," Angela argued.

"Andrew, drive to the field where we collected young caribou," Kristina advised.

Andrew nodded and drove the wagon to the location suggested by Kristina. Spreading blankets at the edge of the trees, Angela found her shade and Kathryn found her view. Andrew gallantly served as butler to his sisters' wishes throughout the picnic. Kristina asked for nothing, merely enjoying the peaceful meadow and fresh aromas of spring blossoms.

When it was time to return home, Kristina took the lead in folding and carrying blankets to the wagon while Andrew carried baskets. Angela and Kathryn climbed into the wagon without help, however Andrew offered his hand to Kristina. She smiled at the offer, but as she took Andrew's hand they both froze.

"Are we going?" Kathryn asked the older two, who were not moving at all.

"QUIET!" Andrew ordered. He then listened intently.

Without a word Kristina and Andrew turned back to the meadow and ran toward a cluster of bushes not far from where they had been relaxing. Drawing near to the spot, they slowed; Andrew put his hand out, signaling Kristina to wait. Suddenly there was a growl, the sound a big dog makes, and the bleat of a young animal. Andrew picked up a large stick and circled the bush.

Reaching the far side, Andrew came upon a wolf pulling the leg of a young caribou. The caribou was uncommonly small and had become tangled in the bush. Unable to free itself, it became prey for the wolf. Andrew held his stick firmly and stared into the wolf's eyes. Warily the wolf maneuvered itself between Andrew and the caribou, defending his claim to the prey. Andrew remained motionless but increased his stark, cold glare, intimidating the wolf.

Kristina was unable to see what was happening on the far side of the bush and slipped silently around the side opposite Andrew. Without warning the wolf found himself caught between Andrew and Kristina. The wild animal could sense that Kristina was there but could not risk breaking its contest with Andrew. Glaring back at Andrew, the wolf raised the hair on its back, increasing its threat. Kristina gasped with horror, which ended the stalemate between Andrew and the wolf.

As Kristina audibly drew her breath, the wolf lunged at Andrew. Andrew's reflexes took over as he countered by bringing the stick up sharply under the wolf's chin and twisting it to the right, sending the wolf tumbling to the ground about two meters away. Immediately the wolf returned to its feet and ran for safety, having been overpowered.

Andrew checked the caribou and found it suffering a significant loss of blood and its back leg mangled . The animal was much smaller than the average caribou calf and there was no herd to care for it. "It won't survive," Andrew said softly as he stroked the calf's neck.

"But you will take it to Gunther," Kristina argued.

"No. Wait here," Andrew replied and ran back to the wagon. He returned a moment later with a large knife and as Kristina softly stroked the calf's head Andrew ended its pain.

Kristina began to sob. With the arms of a saint, Andrew lifted Kristina to her feet and held her as they walked back to the wagon. Returning the knife to its place under the seat, Andrew took Kristina by her hand and arm, guiding her onto the seat of their wagon. Her sobbing stopped, but tears continued to flow. Kathryn and Angela studied Kristina's tears curiously but kept a perplexed silence.

When they reached the lodge Andrew quickly jumped down and offered assistance to Kristina. "Thank you," she sighed. "You were right. Thank you for doing what had to be done." She then wrapped her arms around him and hugged him tightly for several seconds. Releasing him, she quickly disappeared into the lodge.

"Please take care of Kristina," Andrew asked his sisters.

Bewildered, they did as he asked while Andrew silently unhitched the horses and returned baskets and blankets to the kitchen.

Andrew and Kristina's relationship changed that day, for they both left their childhood behind with the young caribou. Kathryn recognized the change but said nothing. Ingrid, the nanny, realized that something was different but could not tell what it was. Jonathon recognized that Andrew was now a young man and on the journey home asked "Andrew, I was eleven when I left Katril to discover my place in the world. How would you like to go to school? Possibly even study business and forestry?"

Andrew not only consented to go to a university but looked forward to the challenge. He spent much of the summer reading and preparing. Jonathon took him to the village of Bronktan in mid-August. Driving his two-horse carriage, Jonathon spent most of the daylong journey remembering how he had attended this same school, sleeping in the barn and doing chores for his meals. The school had grown into a small college specializing in business and agriculture. Some classes even included the practices of Jonathon Syzmoor, which were examined in great detail, however with very little favor. Nobody remembered that he had once been a student there. Andrew Grieg was admitted to the school based on his own interview. His relationship to Jonathon was kept confidential under advice of Professor Jorge Tompkon who was the son of the founder of the university and one of few who knew of Jonathon's past attendance.

Andrew's first semester was spent strengthening his talents in math, government, literature, and other basic studies. He quickly advanced to elementary business classes and requested studies in forestry and agriculture. His professors were skeptical of his choice of studies but allowed the unusually heavy class load as long as he kept his grades above average.

As his studies advanced, Andrew recognized a bias in his professors' lectures. When he could return home, he would discuss the lecture topics with his grandfather who disputed almost every bias with true business experience. Andrew would then return to school and express his newly acquired point of view to the professors. Most of the professors grew exasperated with Andrew's challenges as they were unable to overcome the new perspective he presented, a business ethic of basic simplicity and grace.

Professor Tompkon recognized Andrew's discussions as a reflection of the practices of the Syzmoor Innehav. "You should be careful to discuss but not promote attitudes of your grandfather," Professor Tompkon advised.

"I do not understand, sir," Andrew challenged. "Jonathon Syzmoor would never enter into a contract nor promote any business practice that did not benefit all parties equally."

"But there was a time when he sought only to accumulate wealth and did nothing for his community," Professor Tompkon argued.

"I have heard this, sir. However it has been my personal experience that Mister Syzmoor cares greatly for his community. In fact it is suspected that he secretly finances activities of *The Woodsman*."

"You might be correct Mister Grieg. However, consider at all times that the halls of a university remember hard times and see only how powerful Mister Syzmoor has grown in recent years. As for his relationship with the legendary

Woodsman . . . well, you are probably the only person at this institution who might harbor any thought that the two men could relate to one another." Professor Tompkon smiled and strolled away, leaving Andrew speechless.

That evening Andrew confronted his best friend, Adam, with a question. "Can generosity generate wealth and power?"

Adam, who was studying business and law, laughed. "Absolutely, my naive friend. For out of generosity comes debt, those you give to now owe you. From debt comes power, you now have power over those you gave service to. And from power comes wealth."

"But what if the generosity were anonymous and no debt was harbored?" Andrew argued.

"Only a fool would give and expect nothing in return," Adam responded. "Either that or a man who already had such power that he could not gain or desire an ounce more."

Andrew considered what Adam said and thought quietly, "A man such as my grandfather."

"Adam, do you think my grandfather could be in league with *The Woodsman*?"

"What could the Syzmoor Innehav possibly gain from such a relationship?"

"I said my grandfather, not his business."

"Are they not one and the same? How could you separate them?" Adam smirked and returned to his own studies.

Andrew thought about his grandfather, the man he knew, the man who had raised him. Turning back to his books, Andrew returned to his studies.

A week before Mid-Winter in Andrew's nineteenth year, he arrived at the Syzmoor manor late in the evening. It was Winter Break at the university and the young man had great news. More importantly he was mentally prepared to discuss this news with his grandfather. As Andrew rode up to the stable, next to the manor, Jonathon was just stepping into his sleigh on his way to midnight deliveries. Andrew's heart pounded in his throat as he stared at his grandfather cloaked in white. Suddenly his prepared speech disappeared, indeed he could find nothing to say.

"Okay, either get in the sleigh or go inside. But you will have to move for I have several deliveries to make." Jonathon held up his hands waiting for a decision. Not sure what to do, Andrew pushed his horse into a stall and jumped into the sleigh. "So how is school?" Jonathon asked quite simply.

"You are *The Woodsman*?!" Andrew exclaimed, filled with confusion and uncertainty. "You ARE *The Woodsman*!" he repeated realizing what was happening.

"Yes. Now, how is school?"

The sleigh flew through forests followed by a cloud of snow and ice. Jonathon delivered blankets, clothes, wood, potatoes and meat to three homes in three villages. Andrew found the journey quite exhilarating and began to ask questions on the final stretch toward home. "Grandfather, these families you visit, where do you get their names?"

"Father Patrick leaves notes in a box reserved for the Woodsman. Priests from other villages have learned to send requests through Father Patrick, as well. Nicholas leaves a few whenever he visits."

"Nicholas?" Andrew asked, growing a bit uneasy.

"You will meet him, if you wish." Jonathon chuckled slightly until he noticed how Andrew's hands were getting fidgety. "You have something else on your mind?"

"I have asked Kristina to be my wife. She and Hors have both said YES!! Now, I think you and I need to talk."

"Can we talk in my study with a glass of brandy?"

Andrew smiled and nodded that this would be a better idea. Once the animals had been stabled and brushed, and the sleigh tucked away, Jonathon and Andrew retired to the study. Jonathon poked the fire and added two logs for fuel. Soon the fireplace radiated warmth and the two men sat, each with a short glass of brandy to warm them inside. This was the first time Jonathon had shared a brandy with his grandson.

"So you are going to marry Kristina? Excellent. What do we need to talk about?"

"I will be finishing school in five months. It has been my desire to work with you. I know we have never talked about it, but you will need to retire some day and I would like to be able to assume your roles at head of The Syzmoor Innehav."

"Nothing would make me happier nor more proud than to hand over the reins of Syzmoor Innehav to you when you are ready. When you finish school, you must then begin your education. I would put you in the field working at the mills for a year, maybe two. Then you can accompany me on my sales travels and business meetings until I am ready to release the reins to you."

There was a long silence as both men sipped their brandy and stared into the fire. Andrew finally summoned the courage to ask, "And what about *The Woodsman*?"

"I will keep this very short. You are the reason for the birth of *The Woodsman*." Andrew looked very puzzled, Jonathon continued. "On your first night in this house, when your mother had become ill, you saved some food for your friends, the Metzer's. Since the death of my Kathryn, I had been living behind a wall. Not even living really, just working without any real sensation of life. Your actions at the dinner table that night knocked down the wall that surrounded me and I began to see how much damage I had done through my neglect. Through you, a door opened and my soul was set free. I was given a reason to live, a real reason to embrace life again. I delivered food to the Metzer's that night and have been delivering food, wood, clothing, blankets, and more ever since. The Westmend Innehav pays for supplies, but because of you, I became *The Woodsman*."

"Will I . . . will I inherit this role as well?"

"That will be entirely up to you. If it interests you then I ask you to ride with me as you did tonight. Experience the job, learn a few secrets first, then decide. But please be mindful that this is a secret. The household staff know because I need their help. No one else needs to know."

Days later, at midwinter celebration, Jonathon introduced

Andrew to Nicholas saying, "My grandson is considering assuming my role as *The Woodsman*."

Nicholas looked deep into Andrew's eyes, burrowing down into his heart, before giving his consent. Andrew expected a supreme endorsement or some proclamation from Nicholas, but Nicholas simply stated, "He is a good man. With Kristina by his side, I feel confident he will serve very well."

During the weeks of winter break Andrew made several trips with *The Woodsman*. Jonathon taught him many tricks about stealth, moving silently, and dealing with big dogs. When Andrew asked about Nicholas, Jonathan smiled and replied, "You will come to know him and appreciate his friendship, with time."

Andrew developed a greater respect for his grandfather as a man and benefactor of the community. He had known in his heart that this man, *The Woodsman*, existed and now he had come to know who his grandfather truly was.

When graduation arrived at the University so did Andrew's sisters, their Aunt Rebecca, Rebecca's husband Ralf, and Jonathon Syzmoor. All of Kristina's family except Peder also made the journey to see Andrew receive his diploma. Andrew Grieg had the strongest contingent of any student at graduation. Their celebration lasted all night and into the morning when Andrew and Kristina had to part until their wedding day.

As his coach passed through Katril, on the way back to the manor, Andrew jumped off. Filled with apprehension mingled with excitement he stepped into his parent's cottage, the cottage where he had been born. This was to be his new home, however finding no food he went to the Metzer's cottage and begged for a loaf of bread. Brit and Jon welcomed Andrew and saw that he left with ample bread, meat, potatoes and other food essentials.

Andrew reported for work at the mill the following

morning. Mister Abram Jacobson, mill manager, informed him that he would teach Andrew operations and Jon Metzer would instruct him on timber practices. Jon had worked with Andrew's father and had a great many stories to share about Marc. Through these ongoing stories, Andrew acquired a new appreciation for who his parents were and how important they had been to the village of Katril.

Jonathon had instructed Abram to treat Andrew fairly, without favoritism, but to work him harder than the other men. "See that he has every opportunity to learn and show no leniency on his behalf." When Abram was not pushing Andrew, Jon Metzer kept the young man busy. The single problem with his schedule was a lack of time for making arrangements for his upcoming wedding. Knowing the work load that Jonathon had pushed on Andrew, Rebecca refused to help, forcing everything back on Jonathon.

Having no one to assist him, Jonathon began making plans to transport the family, staff, and friends from Katril to the lodge in Bradsvald for a Mid-Summer Wedding Celebration. This businessman who controlled the largest enterprise in Northern Scandinavia was overwhelmed with details. Jonathon was never satisfied with arrangements until every person had a comfortable seat in a carriage or on horseback, both going and returning, including storage for all luggage and other packages. Jonathon also made a few unusual arrangements with Mister Jacobson at the mill.

"You want to be leaving the mill now?" Mister Jacobson challenged when Andrew requested time off for his wedding. "You only just started and we are coming into our busy season. No, I see no reason for you to take a week's leave of absence. We have plenty of young women here you can marry. You find one tomorrow and get married this Sunday as you planned. Then you will still be here to return to work on Monday."

"Sir," Andrew replied, his voice was crystal clear and his eyes cold and fixed. "Sir, I am traveling to Bradsvald on Wednesday to wed Miss Kristina Anders on Thursday. I will return to work on Monday next. This was the arrangement made with the owner of this mill prior to my employment. Will you honor this arrangement or should I seek other employment?"

"Oh sir, you quite misunderstood my intent," Abram replied. "It is not I who offered this opportunity but the owner of this mill. It was his suggestion made to me last week."

"And his opinion aside, Sir, is it your position that I may return to work as planned or should I seek employment elsewhere?"

"You may return to work as you suggest with one condition, young sir. That your new bride brings you lunch on your first day back so I may meet her myself."

"Thank you, Mister Jacobson." Andrew smiled and returned to his duties, contemplating how he was to deal with his grandfather.

Adam, Andrew's best friend and roommate from the university, was best man. On the day of the wedding, Hannah, the bride's mother, told Adam to get Andrew out of the way. The two young men went exploring. With the sun lingering in its journey across the sky both young men lost track of time. They arrived back at the lodge just in time to get dressed and present themselves before a very nervous Father Patrick.

Andrew was dressed in traditional Dundas, which included woolen shorts, white calf-high hose, a white silk shirt and a vest decorated with symbols of his father's family, plus the image of a reindeer beside a sleigh as his own symbol. This was his father's vest, worn by his father before him, and his father before him. He was a handsome and muscular young man ready to accept responsibilities of the entire world, or at least his new world. Adam was dressed in similar attire. Both men followed Father Patrick through a tunnel in the shrubbery behind the lodge. After speaking with the Metzers and other close friends, Andrew stood and waited for his bride to appear.

A bell chimed in the corridor, Andrew fixed his eyes on the tunnel he had just passed through. Kristina appeared riding a pure white reindeer led by her father. She wore a white cotton dress with silver flowers embroidered around the lower half of the skirt. This was the same dress her mother and grandmother had worn. A crown of summer flowers decorated with silver spoons rested on her head, jingling as the reindeer proceeded. The noise of the spoons knocking together was to have chased away evil spirits, but the music of Kristina's spoons filled the air with joy and laughter.

Andrew looked into her eyes and never saw the reindeer or any of the other attendants also arriving on reindeer, or calves running around sharing in the joy of the party. Kristina and Andrew had been playmates since the age of four, they had explored the vast holdings of the Syzmoor Innehav together, and they had discovered one another in the midst of a tragedy. Today they began a journey that would not only change their lives but embrace the lives of countless family members and friends.

Guests chuckled at reindeer calves bouncing everywhere they should not have gone. Father Patrick wanted to laugh as well, but he was extremely nervous as he began the service. Standing in front of him was Nicholas, the Bishop of Myra, and close personal friend of both families. Nicholas smiled and nodded his head slightly giving Father Patrick the confidence to proceed without hesitation. Nicholas' bride, Natasha, also attended but was quickly lost assisting with work that always accompanies an event such as this.

Feasting, music, and celebration continued late into the night until the sun barely brushed the horizon and began its climb toward the days when it would never be seen. The wedding couple never went to bed that night. Instead, they gathered considerable left over food, which they carried to a small community of Sami reindeer breeders camping nearby. Kristina and Andrew were toasted by the Sami and Andrew learned more about reindeer in their brief visit than Gunther had been able to teach him over several years.

Arriving at their cottage in Katril, the newly married Griegs found the entry lined with evergreen trees, part of an ancient Swedish custom, eight in total. "Are you planning on having a lot of children?" Kristina smiled as she brushed her hands across the small trees. Andrew shook his head trying to shake off the prospect of so many children.

That night, as the couple listened to the silence of the forest and Katril, Andrew rolled over and shared an important secret with his bride. "Kristina, I have been trying to find a time to tell you something and I think this is as private a moment as we will find for a while."

Kristina looked at her groom, her eyes sparkling. With a mischievous grin she taunted her tender young husband, "Are you about to tell me that you turn into a wolf when the moon is full?"

"No, nothing so gruesome. My grandfather is *The Woodsman* and I am training to continue this service."

"*The Woodsman*? You mean Grandfather Jonathon is the one who sneaks into peoples' homes at night and leaves wood and blankets and food?"

"Yes. I do as well."

"I don't think I like this. What if someone should catch you? What if you should fall and hurt yourself, in the middle of the forest in the middle of the night?" Kristina's voice was no longer a taunting whisper but was becoming frantic.

"I am not saying this could not happen. It never has. We go out late at night and return a few hours later. I lose some sleep however it is invigorating, almost magical. We only go out a few nights a week."

Kristina looked at Andrew squarely. In a calm voice she declared, "I do not like this but I do understand. I understand the need and all the good your grandfather has done, and you will do. I will support you because I am your wife. I do not like this and I will worry the entire time you are gone!"

They lay back down in their bed, Andrew holding his bride close to his heart.

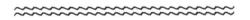

Andrew continued his training at both mills, in Katril and Bradsvald, and in forests with Jon Metzer. When working in the northern region he and Kristina stayed in the lodge, surrounded by Kristina's family, which helped to keep Kristina's spirits up during the long hours Andrew was away. Andrew also accompanied his grandfather on many outings as *The Woodsman*. Kristina understood the importance of *The Woodsman* to the community, but she never liked Andrew's leaving in the middle of the night. She always breathed a sigh of relief as she welcomed him back into their bed.

When a massive ice storm struck Jorstad, near Bradsvald, Jonathon and Andrew were the first rescuers to reach the village. The priest in Jorstad sent a letter to a priest in the next village asking for help from *The Woodsman*. The letter traveled quickly from village to village until it was given to Father Patrick in Katril. Father Patrick did not know how to get in touch with *The Woodsman* in an emergency, so he delivered the letter to Jonathon. Father Patrick was surprised to find Jonathon moving timbers and taking care of injured residents in the devastated village. "My friend has influenza and could not come so I am taking his place. Also, my mills cannot work without the labors of men from this village. I must do what I can to get them back to work," Jonathon explained. Nobody challenged this claim for it was true to Jonathon's nature - strictly business. Andrew kept the charade alive as he continued to work with men from the mills recovering the village, long after Jonathon left. *The Woodsmen*, two of them, provided significant support for repairing a broken community.

Abram Grieg was born eighteen months into Andrew and Kristina's marriage, arriving mid-winter, Christmas Day 1846. Nicholas gave Jonathon only one name to care for that evening, Kristina Grieg. Jonathon was true to his task and went joyfully to his grandson's cottage. Unlike other visits, *The Woodsman* knocked at the door and waited for his grandson to invite him to enter. While Jonathon visited with Kristina, Andrew held his son, silently staring down into the tiny face of a new generation. Andrew's heart beat steady and strong. His breathing was easy yet filled with intent and his mind traveled rapidly through time as he tried to foresee what he must do to provide for his growing family. Money was not an issue for this small family, but involvement in each other's lives was critical. Andrew was training to take over the Syzmoor Innehav, an empire of growing proportion and responsibility. He was training to become the second generation *Woodsman*, a servant to this vast community and Nicholas. Now, he was a father, which at that moment was far more important than all the rest.

Not long after Abram's birth, Jonathon saw a change in the way Andrew conducted business. Pleased with the changes and growing maturity Andrew showed, Jonathon passed on greater responsibilities in running the Syzmoor Innehav, and greater freedoms as well. Andrew enjoyed these freedoms and began following his childhood dream of raising caribou.

Gunther Hansen was training his two sons to assume responsibilities of managing game in the northern regions and breeding reindeer. Caribou bred for domestic purposes are called reindeer. Whenever possible Andrew would join the Hansen boys working with the reindeer. They were both much younger than he. The boys thought it rather comical that their father's employer, one of the richest men in the country, was cleaning reindeer stalls and brushing down the animals right beside them. Andrew found the work invigorating and rewarding but not always refreshing. Often, the heir to the Syzmoor Innehav would return to the lodge reeking of sweat, dirty straw, and animals. Hannah, Kristina's mother, would not allow him into the lodge until he had cleaned up at the pump outside, just like the mill workers.

One Summer afternoon in 1848, Andrew returned to the lodge filled with delight. He had a young reindeer with him, an addition for their small collection at the manor house. As he entered the lodge, with the reindeer in his arms, Hannah greeted Andrew with his new daughter in her arms. Kristina had delivered their second child, a young lady named Marianne, several weeks sooner than expected. Their return home was delayed a week until mother and daughter were ready to travel in comfort. Abram, now nineteen months old, was charged with keeping the calf quiet. It was a long journey home.

~~~~~~~~~~~~~~~~

Jonathon Syzmoor found great pleasure and reward as *The Woodsman*. Midnight journeys were invigorating and peaceful. Having his grandson by his side much of the time was a source of great pride. Nicholas took advantage of Andrew's help and asked more from Jonathon, rather Jonathon and Andrew.

Jonathon pulled the sleigh to a stop in the middle of the forest after completing the last of five difficult deliveries. Looking around at the familiar location lit by moonlight reflected off freshly fallen snow, Jonathon turned his gaze to his grandson, Andrew.

"You have been riding with me for several years, since before you and Kristina were married," Jonathon began. "You have told me that Kristina does not really like your nighttime excursions, even though she appreciates the work we do, and she does welcome you back to bed. You have proven yourself very capable in the management of running our business holdings. Are you ready to take the reins of this sleigh?"

Andrew took a deep breath. Looking at his grandfather's face for the message he anticipated longingly yet feared, he replied, "It has been an honor, and an even greater pleasure to ride in this sleigh with you, Grandfather." Andrew paused and drew another deep breath slowly. "And when you are ready to release the reins of this marvelous sleigh, I would be honored to take them."

"My first ride with Nicholas ended in this glade," Jonathon mused. "That was many years ago and many, many midnight visits. You will enjoy his company when he rides with you. I must share with you now the three things that Nicholas shared with me at the end of our first journey together." Jonathon took a breath and loosed the reins so White Star and Odin could relax. As they shook the cold from their shoulders Jonathon commented, almost absent mindedly, "Those two have pulled this sleigh many nights. They have been fabulous companions."

Realizing he was off track Jonathon continued, "The first

thing you must always remember is that we did not create poverty or need. The poor have been with us since the dawn of civilization and while we can improve the lot of those we touch, we cannot eliminate poverty or need. Second, you have many responsibilities. You are a father, two delightful children and a third on the way. You are a husband, and you are successfully learning the management of a vast business empire."

Jonathon pulled his pocket watch from his vest and opened the back exposing the many gears ticking fragilely with one another. "Just like this fine timepiece, you must balance all of your responsibilities. If one part of your life begins to overshadow your other responsibilities, everything will stop. You must keep balance in your life - not an easy task with long nights such as tonight. Nicholas has always been sensitive to this and helps me stay balanced. I feel he will do this for you as well, if you allow him to.

"And finally, expect nothing from your efforts - as *The Woodsman* or in business, but especially as *The Woodsman*. Some people will take the help you provide and gain nothing but one warm meal or blazing fire. Some people will take what you give them and when it is exhausted come looking for more; they strive to survive on handouts. Then there are those who will take your assistance and climb out of their troubles. They will build a new life on the foundation you provide and then begin to help others. You may believe, at first, that you can identify what will happen by looking at the cottages we visit, but I assure you we cannot. Look at the cottages and learn what is important to those we serve, but never assume you know what their tomorrow will bring, with or without our help."

Jonathon looked at Andrew and then cast his eyes through the shadows surrounding their sleigh. In the silence he handed the reins to Andrew with a final word, "This sleigh actually belongs to Nicholas, or once did, but as he gave you his blessing long ago these reins are now yours. I will continue to serve as *Woodsman* as long as I am able, but the reins now belong to you."

Andrew could find nothing to say but took the reins from his grandfather. Suddenly the weight of the leather straps seemed unbearably heavy. Attempting to show his worthiness, Andrew tried to draw a deep breath of air, finding his throat and lungs closed. Silently he exhaled and lifted the reins. All he could manage was a light shake, however Odin and White Star immediately stepped off with one another. Andrew quietly began to breathe again and the sleigh lifted off the snow, leaving a frosted plume behind them without any tracks. Jonathon sat back and smiled. Turning his head to the left he imagined he saw a sleigh carrying a man in a long red cape. The man waved as his sleigh pulled by two reindeer flew silently through the shadows.

~~~~~~~~~~~~~~~~~~~~

Andrew and Kristina moved into the Manor House before their third child, a daughter, was born on their fifth wedding anniversary, Mid-Summer 1850. Kristina suffered a difficult labor bringing Hannah into the world. She was named for her grandmother.

While the summer of 1850 was filled with the joy of a new baby, autumn found Jonathon declining in strength. Returning home with Andrew from an evening of Woodsman deliveries, Jonathon felt very weak. Andrew sent for the doctor immediately, but the doctor only confirmed what all knew. Jonathon would have one last journey in his wonderful sleigh.

The funeral service for Jonathon was moved, just prior to its start, from the chapel in Katril into the square so all in attendance could hear and take part. On a brisk October afternoon, Andrew delivered an inspiring eulogy proclaiming his grandfather to be "an egotistical self-righteous pain" and describing his incredible passion for his community, family, and bride.

At the close of the service Nicholas approached Andrew. Tears rolled gently down Nicholas' cheek, disappearing into his beard. "A beautiful tribute, young Sir. I too will miss him for I have lost a brother. However, the living are still in need."

Slowly Nicholas reached into his cape, drew out a list of names, and pressed it into *The Woodsman*'s hand.

With a heavy sigh Andrew held the paper and watched Nicholas walk away. "Can you not visit just once without leaving a list?" Andrew thought to himself. "The poor and needy will always be with us, but why tonight?" With a heavy heart he unfolded the paper and read the following names: "In the family Syzmoor, Rebecca Syzmoor Larsen; In the family Grieg, Andrew, Angela, and Kathryn. Please take special care that all members of this splendid and remarkable family receive the most humble blessings of their dear servant Nicholas." Andrew looked out and saw Nicholas tending to the needs of everyone on the list. Andrew's list was being cared for.

A week after his grandfather's funeral, Andrew stepped into his sleigh and lifted the reins. He had not yet put on his gloves so he felt cool leather resting across his palms. This was the first time he had been out as *The Woodsman* since Jonathon's death and the young man felt very uneasy. Exhausted before he began, he fell back into the seat and let his chin fall to his chest. Breathing was difficult and tears began to well up and spill down his cheek.

Shuffling his feet with discomfort, Andrew felt something against his heel. Leaning over, he found Jonathon's staff. *The Woodsman's Staff*. Lifting it he recalled how he held it as his grandfather took his final breaths. The soft glow of its candle-lit crystal filled the room with a peaceful warmth. Andrew had put the staff beneath the seat for Jonathon's last sleigh ride.

Reaching into his vest pocket, Andrew retrieved a wooden match and lit the candle beneath the crystal. That remarkable crystal. As it began to glow, he remembered when Jonathon first demonstrated its remarkable warmth. First snows of winter had just begun to fall and he found his grandfather working on this remarkable walking stick.

"Do you remember the crystal you gave me before your wedding?" Jonathon asked. Andrew shrugged his shoulders, not sure whether he remembered or not. "Watch." Jonathon had carved out the top of his walking staff so that it was hollow in the middle and open on one side. He easily slipped a candle inside and it held securely in a lower hollow below the crystal mounted on the top. When the candle was lit, the crystal began to glow, softly at first, it then magnified the small light of the candle. The glow was soft yet filled the room and seemed to wrap around objects dispelling all shadows. "You could easily light a cottage with this crystal and not disturb the sleeping occupants."

"Would you like some company tonight?"

The lightness of the voice lifted Andrew's spirit and his chin. Raising his head he saw Kristina wrapped in a cape and ready for an evening of riding in a most splendid sleigh.

"What about the children?" Andrew asked, allowing his lips to smile.

"Mister Woodsman, have you forgotten the hour? Everyone in the house is sound asleep and I have left a note in the kitchen should anyone waken before we return. Why don't you slide over just a bit and make room for me?"

Andrew blew out the candle in *The Woodsman's Staff* and carefully placed it beneath the sleigh bench, as his grandfather had done so many times. Andrew then slid over, just a bit, and Kristina snuggled next to him, looping her arm around his. No longer fearing the journey ahead, *The Woodsman* snapped the reins and two powerful reindeer pulled the sleigh across the courtyard and onto the public road. Not a track was left for the sleigh rose above the snow and ice leaving only a cloud behind which covered all traces of its journey.

Silently, the reindeer and sleigh slipped through the vast countryside making three stops at the homes of people in quiet need. A list containing these homes was given to *The Woodsman* by Father Peter, of the church in Katril. Kristina had never been on a ride such as this and while the night was romantic, the sights tugged relentlessly at her heart. Andrew did most of the work at each stop, but Kristina could not resist covering up the children and saying a prayer for their welfare. Each time she felt the cottage begin to warm while she waited at the door watching *The Woodsman*, her husband, rebuild meager fires and then carefully close the door behind them.

Andrew pulled his bride close to him, relaxing the reins so the reindeer could trot home after their last visit. Quietly, she put her head on his shoulder and gazed at the crystal sky above them. "Is it always this clear when you go out?" she asked in amazement.

"Only in the winter and only if it is not snowing," Andrew chuckled slightly. "Some nights I cannot see the road so I tell the team to 'take me home' and somehow they do it."

The Woodsman tradition came close to ending that night. Instead it was enriched by the love and compassion of *The Woodsman's* wife. Kristina rode with Andrew often, providing the weather was clear and the children were sleeping soundly.

~~~~~~~~~~~~~~~~~~~~~~~~~

Andrew did not fare as well stepping into his grandfather's shoes in The Syzmoor Innehav. Jonathon Syzmoor built a vast empire promoting more efficient land use, modern practices in forestry, tenant land utilization, business subsidy, and small team management. Jonathon pioneered new concepts of conservation and preservation in a world that traditionally ravaged the land and abused people. He promoted new practices as easily as taking a breath of fresh air. Andrew had studied at his side for years, observing, assisting, and asking questions. Yet, the burden which Jonathon carried so lightly now crushed this young man.

During the first three months, late October through mid-January, Andrew met with every tenant, crew chief, business owner / partner, and supervisor within the Syzmoor Innehav. He had met each of these men previously, in the company of his grandfather, but now he was in charge. When meeting with owners, partners, and managers of the businesses the Innehav subsidized, Andrew took Adam with him. Adam had been his roommate at the university, was married to his sister Angela, and was the attorney with oversight of these many entities. Andrew had always placed a significant trust in Adam's counsel and advice, but now he learned to rely on Adam's business expertise as well.

There were thirty-seven tenants on Innehav owned land, six of which were secondary where another tenant managed their property as part of his own. As Andrew visited with each tenant, primary and secondary, he considered hiring someone to oversee the issues with this part of the Innehav. He discussed tenant management with six men, not telling them his plans nor that he was considering them as this manager. Five times he became aware of personalities that could lead to more trouble than he had now. The sixth gentleman would have been an excellent manager but already had more to do than he could manage without the help of his wife. Andrew remembered his grandfather's comments about this family; the young man had inherited an estate overburdened by debt. Jonathan also predicted this family could become good and trusted friends. He was correct. Andrew resigned himself to continue to care for the tenants and their occasional problems.

Andrew had studied business and forestry at the university and had learned a great deal from his grandfather. Most of the Syzmoor Innehav holdings were in forests and timber, holdings the young executive was comfortable managing. The one issue that taxed Andrew was the combination of the vast expanse he now owned and tracts he managed for others. In the first three months he barely had time to visit all sites. The distance required several trips lasting eight to ten days and nights, time he traveled without companionship. His grandfather cherished these times of quiet travel, but Andrew wanted to complete the journeys and return home to his family. During the course of the first round of visits he found three sites where the local overseer was not doing his job as Andrew would have it done. Each man was warned of problems found and told that if he did not comply with instructions, Andrew would find someone who would. Two of the men became hostile, adding to Andrew's concerns.

Being in charge of the Syzmoor Innehav did have its rewards. Mid-Winter was a special time of year for Andrew and Kristina. They sent invitations from the Syzmoor Manor which surprised many people in the surrounding counties, for Jonathon Syzmoor had always kept Christmas very quietly, in respectful solitude. Andrew and Kristina decorated the manor not just for Mid-Winter but for Christmas and the doors were opened to all guests. Andrew brought in a large tree which stood in the foyer and was decorated with streamers, candles, fruit balls, and other brightly colored nicknacks. The open house was held on Christmas Day, emphasizing the birth of Christ and acknowledging the birth of the new generation in the manor.

Nicholas visited the open house on his way home explaining to Andrew, "I have been out all night, and like you I wish to get back to my bride. If you do this again next year, I should like to bring Natasha. She loves decorated trees and joyful gatherings."

Before Andrew could reply, Abram ran into Nicholas' legs, almost knocking him over. Kristina was not far behind the young man, carrying Hannah. Nicholas immediately reached out and took six-month-old Hannah in his arms. She focused her eyes on his smile and studied his face with great intensity. "Well, young lady, do I get approval from such inspection or do I have a crumb in my beard?" Nicholas smiled and Hannah beamed with delight.

Seeing Nicholas' exhaustion in his eyes, Andrew took Hannah and thanked him for taking the time to come by. Nicholas shook his hand firmly, did not leave any lists, and proceeded to visit with other guests for just over an hour. Nicholas disappeared as quietly as he had arrived.

Winter melted into spring, as it always does, and markets in Katril and Landsvardt came back to life just as the beech and oak trees did. While visiting in Landsvardt, Kristina overheard a conversation in the market which caused her some concern. That evening she sat with her husband, who was preparing for midnight deliveries.

"Andrew, does it matter who delivers the food and blankets you leave?"

"What do you mean?" Andrew asked, his face wrinkled in confusion.

"In the market today I overheard two ladies discussing families you had visited. It seems there are others who are trying to take credit for your efforts."

"I have never thought about who gets credit, just so long as people who need help find it," Andrew replied. But the thought of others taking credit for his work began to fester.

Many months later Andrew returned from an evening of deliveries and after stabling the reindeer he felt someone waiting for him. Leaving the stable, he found Nicholas waiting in the courtyard with his sleigh and reindeer. Moments later Andrew was enjoying his first ride in a sleigh pulled by lentävä poro, flying reindeer, and on his way to Alapuolella Pohjantähti (the Village at the North Pole). Nicholas stopped before reaching home to help a young caribou trapped in a bush. During the rescue Andrew noticed some trees with very unusual bark. The bark was thick, very thick, but unusually smooth. While Nicholas freed the caribou, Andrew cut a small branch to take with him.

Andrew's first visit to Nicholas' home was educational and fun. Returning home, Andrew made certain he had the unusual tree branch. Nicholas admired this stick but could not understand why Andrew wanted it. He also brought the caribou Nicholas had freed, a rambunctious calf who presented an effervescent personality and boundless energy. The caribou earned the named Rolfh, because that was the sound that filled the air every time he opened his mouth.

Andrew spent considerable time in the days that followed caring for Rolfh and working with the branch. He cut the branch into sections about the width of his hand. The wood was incredibly dense and the bark thick and leathery. Abram was playing with a short piece of the branch and actually pulled the bark off the wood in a single piece, much like a ring. Seeing the flexibility and durability of the bark, Andrew took another piece of the branch and began carving off just the bark in various designs, doing his best to remove only the bark and not cut into the wood. Working with the tree branch, he came to recognize this wood as being the source of some beautiful art he had seen in different villages. Unfortunately he had only the one small sample.

Not long after his visit with Nicholas, Andrew was surveying an older piece of land that his grandfather had purchased for its furniture grade timber. While marking trees for harvest he found a small grove of the same type of trees he had discovered while rescuing Rolfh. His heart beat with growing excitement as he collected a number of branches between one and two inches in diameter. Each branch was cut with care so as to not damage the host tree. When he returned two days later to dress the cuts with protective sealer, he found the tree had already sealed each cut preventing infection by insects.

Andrew cut the branches into lengths about the width of his hand, thicker branches a bit shorter. He then set to work with a penknife, carefully carving the letters "SYL" out of the bark. At his desk Andrew carefully printed the words "Share Your Life" on strips of paper. On the next journey of *The Woodsman* Andrew asked Kristina to place one of the etched pieces and a strip of paper where the family might find it but not lose it. Kristina was impressed with his new signature.

After a few years almost every one of The Woodsman's sticks changed. The wood would shrink just slightly releasing the bark which would slip off the wooden core. Owner's of these treasured mementoes found that some wooden cores carried the image of the letters in the bark and some did not. It was speculated that those with clearer etchings were done when *The Woodsman* was worried about something and those with clear cores were done when he was more relaxed. When Andrew heard these stories he smiled and became very careful of how his penknife did its work, using great care to not touch the wood. Nicholas smiled with delight when he heard this story, offering "I can always get more of this wood should you ever need it."

From the time Andrew met his first caribou, at the age of four years, he had a love of these remarkable animals and showed a true talent for working with them. Gunther Hansen was jealous of Andrew's ability to walk up to caribou in the wild and could never understand why an entire pen of reindeer would leave the feeding trough and walk over to Andrew. Andrew also had a love for his grandfather's white reindeer. They were uncommon and beautiful. Andrew kept reindeer at the manor from the time he took over the estate from Jonathon. He often had more reindeer than horses.

Introducing Rolfh into the reindeer stable caused a bit of crowding, but there were two other reindeer his age. This caused Andrew to consider his reindeer for a new purpose. He had been relying on Gunther to breed the reindeer at the northern bondgard and then bring selected animals to the manor. During the spring months following the arrival of Rolfh, Andrew fenced a parcel of land next to the manor, about three acres, and established a breeding program for personal use.

Andrew had wanted to try selective breeding of reindeer since the time of his wedding, when he and Kristina visited the Sami near the lodge. Sami were successfully breeding for strength and size, but Andrew also wanted colour and personality. Andrew worked with each of his reindeer, individually studying their personality, physical strengths, endurance and purity of colour. When mating season arrived he would restrict males' access to only certain females. The third generation of selective breeding produced incredibly strong animals with stable temperaments and pleasant personalities. White colours were more common than in the wild or at Gunther's farm but were still not absolute. The darker reindeer were used for family trips while the whites were used by *The Woodsman*.

While attempting to get more white deer from his breeding program, Andrew wrote a scholarly paper. He sent copies to several universities asking for help. Most of the replies to his inquiries suggested he spend more time with the Sami, however there was a result Andrew had not expected. He began receiving letters from men and women who were inspired by his paper to begin their own breeding programs. Andrew answered each letter personally, referring requests for purchase to Gunther.

One letter so intrigued Andrew that after replying he put it aside to share with Nicholas. After silently reading the letter, Nicholas burst out laughing, "I love this man's spirit. How did you reply to his inquiry?"

"I explained to him that the flying reindeer he sought were properly called 'lentävä poro' and based on his address, which you can see is in Scotland, he would not be able to successfully breed this unique variety of reindeer."

"May I keep this letter?" Nicholas asked, smiling at Andrew's comment.

"Of course, but why?" Andrew replied, his face wrinkled with curiosity.

"I think I should write a letter to the gentleman myself and offer him an opportunity to meet my lentävä poro personally. His belief could be quite contagious, don't you think?"

Andrew met a surprise as he approached the front door of the manor in mid-October 1854, his tenth year serving as *The Woodsman*. Eight-year-old Abram waited for him, dressed in boots, warm clothes and a cape that was a bit too large. "I would like to ride with *The Woodsman*" Abram announced.

Andrew looked down at his son and quickly reviewed his route for the evening. It would be long, but there were only two stops to make. The weather had been clear that afternoon and it promised to be a mild night. *The Woodsman* then ran his eyes up and down the self-invited companion and smiled, "Your cape is a bit large."

"I will leave it in the sleigh when we make our stops," young Abram announced.

"Go ahead, let him ride with you," Kristina laughed. "He has been looking forward to an evening with *The Woodsman*."

Andrew pursed his lips and looked down at Abram sternly, "You must never speak of the places we visit nor of what you see. These are private matters and should never be discussed openly."

"Father," Abram said with a bit of exasperation, "I have never revealed your secret."

"Who would you reveal our secret to?" Andrew asked with sudden curiosity.

"The children in school and in Katril often talk about your visits. Many talk as if they know what cottages you are going to visit. I listen but have never added my opinions." Abram then lowered his eyes and continued, "I have been told that I will never see *The Woodsman* because we have no needs."

"Go get in the sleigh; I will be there in a moment," Andrew told the young man as he reached down, turned his son's shoulder with one hand, and opened the door with the other. Turning to his wife he asked, "Are our children being persecuted for our wealth? Do they not know all that we do for the villages?"

"Abram has worked hard to keep your secret," Kristina whispered as she pulled Andrew's cape closed. "He hopes to drive the sleigh one day when you are too old."

Andrew kissed his wife gently and repeated her words, "Too old? Maybe we should get another sleigh from Nicholas and he could have two *Woodsmen*. I am fifteen years younger now than when my grandfather started these insane midnight runs." He pulled the door closed and joined Abram in the sleigh.

That first ride was an experience that showed Abram the best and the worst of man. He saw one home that was humble yet filled with love. Meager appointments revealed a great faith, caring, and concern, not only for the immediate family but for their community as well. Abram picked up a carving done by a member of the household and turned it over in his hand several times before placing it precisely where he found it, amid the knives and shavings.

"You were examining that carving with great attention," Andrew remarked as the cloud of snow and ice chased them toward their next visit.

"I have seen one before, almost identical," Abram replied. "Thomas, a boy in the village got one for his birthday, but I also saw them for sale at the market in Landsvardt. I do not believe Thomas' father could afford the price they were asking in the market. I think whoever carved it gave one to Thomas' father so Thomas could have it for his birthday."

Andrew smiled and shook the reins.

Arriving at the second cottage Abram took a deep breath and gasped. This cottage was in great need of repair and refuse was scattered all around. Abram entered the cottage reluctantly and saw tattered clothing scattered about and unwashed dishes and utensils. Two children huddled on blankets in a corner and their parents stretched out on a broken cot near them. There was no art, no family mementoes, no signs of faith nor friends. While Andrew prepared some meat for the children and spread a new blanket over them, Abram stacked fresh wood in the fire, adding just enough to keep it going without overheating the small cottage.

Abram never said a word, however Andrew noticed a tear on his cheek. "We never judge those whom we serve, we simply serve as best we can," Andrew advised placing a hand on his son's shoulder. Their ride home was quiet.

Abram began taking trips with *The Woodsman* twice each month, providing the weather was not too severe. One January trip the temperature was so cold on a long night that Abram swore he would never go out into the countryside in the cold again. That vow lasted about four days, until the sun warmed the countryside and the family went to visit in Katril.

Four months into Abram's journeys they came to an abrupt halt. Andrew had four names on his list and they were a great distance apart, making for a long night. When they reached the last of the cottages, Andrew carried all of the supplies, except wood. Abram carried the wood, but being very tired he dropped several pieces. As Abram placed the wood he carried into a bin, Andrew nodded his head toward the door, indicating Abram should pick up the wood he dropped. Abram nodded with a slight grin and disappeared quietly out the door.

Minutes later Andrew heard a dog's snarl and stepped to the door as a large mastiff leapt at Abram. Moving as fast as the dog, Andrew shot toward his son slipping the Woodsman's staff under the dog's neck. The dog clenched down on Abram's arm as Andrew snapped the animal back with one forceful jerk. Pulling up on the Woodsman's staff with all his strength, Andrew flung the beast to the side. Leaving his task unfinished and the cottage door open, Andrew grabbed Abram and dropped him in the sleigh.

Their route that night had been a wide loop with the fourth stop being only fourteen kilometers from the manor. Fourteen kilometers of heart beating, breathless, hoof pounding, blinding speed. Andrew laid Abram across the bench and then stood, trying to control the reins with one hand and assure his son with the other. Never had the reindeer run so fast. Never had Andrew asked so much of them.

Arriving at the manor Andrew lifted his son, who was now not quite two thirds the size of a man, and burst inside calling loudly, "KRISTINA! KRISTINA! MISTER STYNGE!" Within seconds the elderly butler appeared and seeing the situation, pulled Andrew into the kitchen. Mister Stynge cleared the table with a single motion and produced a towel for Abram's head. Kristina appeared as the two men were removing Abram's coat. There was no blood, but when Abram rolled up his sleeve the arm was severely bruised and showed signs of a break in the bones.

"I am going for Doctor Smalz," Andrew announced and disappeared.

Doctor Smalz had been taken into the family's confidence about *The Woodsman* when he attended to Jonathon's death. This was one of those rare times when Andrew was glad, for he did not have to explain why they were out in the middle of the night, only what happened. Talking calmly over breakfast, Doctor Smalz announced, "I cannot be certain, yet I believe you, Andrew, broke your son's arm when you pulled the brute off of him. No doubt greater damage would have been suffered had you not. Next time pull with somewhat less force." The doctor smirked as he lifted his cup of tea.

Abram lost much of his appetite for midnight adventure as his arm healed, that is until he completed his university studies at the age of nineteen years.

Kristina continued to ride with *The Woodsman* until they became grandparents. Her diary entries became less frequent when Abram began riding with his father at the age of sixteen. She would frequently yield her seat to their son, so little can be added to this time in Andrew's story. The entries of Kristina continue to show a man who worked very hard, always striving to do what was right for his community even though it might have cost him personally. Which is often the legacy of *The Woodsmen*.

An incident occurred during the Spring of 1859 that caused Andrew to file papers with his attorney in the event an action was filed against him, or *The Woodsman*. After a long day of visiting logging sites Andrew stopped by the mill in Katril. Parched from riding, he invited Fredrick, the mill manager, to join him for an ale while they discussed business of the mill.

While they were enjoying their drink and conversation, a man began yelling from across the tavern. "HEY! Mister Mill Manager, I have not received my pay packet! I am talking to you, Fredrick, and you as well, Mister Grieg. You owe me my pay packet!"

Stumbling from intoxication the man approached the table where Andrew and Fredrick were talking. "Excuse me, Mister Grieg; I will take care of this man," Fredrick said quietly as he stood to meet the man.

Oxn Brendol stood nearly six feet four inches and weighed at least two hundred sixty pounds. He had broad shoulders and a ruddy complexion beneath his scraggy beard. "I want my pay packet!" he screamed as Fredrick stood to meet him.

"I told you earlier I will give you your pay when you are sober enough to sign for it," Fredrick replied calmly.

Oxn grabbed Fredrick by the shirt and lifted him so they were eye to eye, "You owe me for my work. I want my pay packet. Now!"

Andrew stood as Oxn grabbed Fredrick, planting the heel of his boot on the top of Oxn's foot. Oxn dropped Fredrick and took a swing at Andrew, who calmly hooked the drunken man's arm with his own, dropping him to the floor. The tavern owner and another man apologized to Andrew and Fredrick as they carried Oxn out of the tavern.

Returning to their seats Fredrick explained, "He came to work this morning smelling of ale and a bit unsteady. When he moved a stack of lumber, he knocked one of the cutters into the saw. Had the saw been running, it would have killed the cutter instantly. I told Oxn to get out and not return. He did ask for his pay packet and I told him to come back when he could sign for it. Besides, if I gave it to him when he was drunk he would just drink it away and then demand it again to feed his family."

After leaving the tavern Andrew stopped at the chapel in Katril, where he picked up messages for *The Woodsman*. There was a slip of paper which he tucked into his vest pocket without looking at it. In the privacy of his study Andrew pulled the paper and found two names with needs; the second name was the family of Oxn Brendol. He was still staring at the paper when Kristina joined him.

"Something troubling?" she asked.

"A name on this request for service. The man is a drunk and a trouble maker. I wonder if *The Woodsman* should reward his behavior?" Andrew pondered.

"Well," Kristina considered, "is it the man or his family who needs help?"

Andrew thought for a moment and replied, "You are right

and I believe we can meet their needs tonight if you care to ride with me."

Kristina thought out loud, "I haven't been with *The Woodsman* for some time and the manor is quiet. Yes, I believe I would enjoy an evening under the stars." They left quietly, long after dark covered the countryside. The first visit was very simple and took little time. Approaching the Brendol cottage, they were surprised to find a lantern lighted inside. Andrew stopped the sleigh about ten meters from the cottage as was his custom and waited.

At first the cottage was quiet, then they heard Oxn yelling loudly "INGRID! INGRID!" Calls were followed by sounds of tables and chairs crashing and a burst of light. Andrew and Kristina watched as one end of the small cottage immediately became engulfed in flame.

Andrew raced to the door which he found locked. Raising his boot, he put all of his weight into a powerful kick. The door flew open to a horror of flame and smoke. "Three children," Andrew thought about the message, "three children." Taking a deep breath of air, Andrew plunged into the cabin, scanning the sides and corners. He spotted a ladder going to a loft over the parent's bed. Without hesitation *The Woodsman* ran to the ladder, climbed quickly and grabbed feet, blankets, whatever his hands could find. With two children in his arms, Andrew rushed to the door where Kristina took the children.

Turning back to retrieve the third child and mother, Andrew ran into Oxn. "What are you doing in my home?" Oxn bellowed. "This is MY home! You are not welcome here!"

"Mister Brendol, your cottage is on fire! Get your wife out while I try to get your children!" Andrew tried to get Oxn to save himself, but Oxn put his fist to the side of Andrew's head. Andrew fell back several steps. Regaining his balance, he then tried to get around Oxn to save the others. Oxn again tried to hit Andrew, but Andrew was ready, hooking his arm to swing the brute out of the way. Oxn fell to the ground, hitting his head on the fireplace.

Andrew went to the bed where the mother was not

sleeping but was knocked out with multiple bruises on her face. *The Woodsman* shook her until she stirred slightly, then climbed the ladder to find the third child crying. "Come with me, your brothers are outside where it is safe," he coaxed the child. With the child in his arms he pulled the mother to her feet and they stumbled out of the cottage. Fire had spread from the end opposite the beds and now filled two thirds of the walls and roof.

"What about the father?" Kristina asked as Andrew lay the mother on the ground.

Andrew looked into Kristina's eyes and then at the rest of the family on the ground around them. Lowering his head he took a deep breath and softly prayed, "Dear Father in Heaven, do not let this be my last act as *The Woodsman*." Fearful but determined, Andrew plunged back into the burning cottage. Oxn was out cold with a bit of blood on the side of his head. Calling on all of his strength, Andrew lifted the man just as a burning timber crashed into Andrew's arm causing him to drop Oxn. Burning embers lodged on Andrew's sleeve but went unnoticed as he again lifted Oxn, carrying him from the cottage. They had just cleared the cottage door when Andrew's sleeve burst into flame. Andrew dropped the man again as he pulled his cape around his arm extinguishing the blaze.

Kristina looked at Andrew's arm. There was nothing she could do about the seared flesh until they returned home. With his arm wrapped in his cape, Andrew walked around the burning remains of the cottage making certain it would not spread across the ground. He and Kristina then delivered the family to the chapel in Katril. Pounding on the priest's door the couple vanished before he opened his home to a family desperately needing further attention.

Andrew's arm suffered severe burns, but healed after several weeks of care from his wife. Neither Oxn nor his wife could account for their burned cottage or how they arrived at the chapel. The three children smiled gratefully every time they saw Kristina in church or in the market.

Andrew remained true to his grandfather's plans for The Syzmoor Innehav. Under his management the Innehav continued to prosper but grew very little. Andrew realized that he could visit each holding only once in three months so he never actively sought additional holdings or properties. It had taken him years to become accustomed to his responsibilities. He was now able to manage them though not always comfortably.

Remembering lessons from his grandfather on their midnight rides, Andrew kept watch for estates that might be in trouble. Whenever he saw a single light in a window, he looked for a carriage or sleigh which might belong to a doctor or priest and then made inquiry about the family. Six times over his forty-three years, Andrew discovered families in trouble brought on by greed or stupidity but whose failure would not have a significant impact on their community. His efforts on behalf of these families was minimal, seeking primarily to protect the community. Thirteen times he found families and estates which were caught in misfortune through no direct fault of their own and in every case Andrew exerted his influence and resources to save the family, estate, and community. He regretted only one of these actions.

This singular instance began in the early Autumn of 1865 when *The Woodsman* happened upon a burning house. Three children had escaped the blaze, but their father, Axel, was unable to save his wife. The house had been an ancestral home of the wife and all of the family's heritage was lost in the blaze.

"I was working late," Axel explained, "trying to find the resources to rebuild a farm I recently acquired. The farm is home to a widow with four children. She is a good woman and is looking to me for help. I must have fallen asleep and the tobacco in my pipe fell on the papers. I got the children out. By the time I got to my wife, our room was engulfed in flame. It was directly above my study."

Andrew helped the children get settled in the barn and the next day sent his attorney to check on the estate. Banks would not help the man for he had mortgaged his property heavily and had not been making payments. "I was trying to rebuild a farm I recently acquired," Andrew remembered the man telling him. Against advice of his attorney and thinking only of the children's loss, Andrew purchased the debts from the bank and financed rebuilding the family home. The house was not as grande as the one they once had, but it was a very comfortable home.

Six months after the death of his wife, Axel married the widow from the farm he had acquired. The man sent a letter to Andrew's attorney stating "My household has now doubled in size since your generous assistance. I now ask for your assistance in building an addition to my house for my new wife and children." Andrew's initial reaction was an absolute NO, he would not add to the house. Pondering the situation before writing the reply to his attorney, however, he remembered *share your life without expectation*. His grandfather's advice haunted him until he consented to the addition.

Two years later another letter came from Axel stating, "a man in my employ has met an untimely death. He has left a young wife and one child, age two years. His own home is in very poor condition and I am requesting assistance in its restoration."

Andrew instructed his attorney to make quiet inquiry about Axel's affairs, both current and for the past ten years. The inquiry revealed that the man had come into his first marriage without any resources of his own and he had nearly bankrupted his wife's estate. He was, at that time, having relations with the widow on the farm he acquired and whom he later married. Suspicions were strong that he was also having relations with the widow for whom he now sought support. Axel was currently three months behind in his mortgage payments to the Syzmoor Innehav. Andrew's reply was "Dear Sir, you are behind in your mortgage payments and have shown no character which would give us reason to expect correction of this condition. You are hereby ordered to vacate the premises owned by The Syzmoor Innehav immediately. Your wife and children may stay in their home until arrangements can be made for suitable housing. Should you be found in residence on any Syzmoor Innehav properties you will be incarcerated immediately and held until such time as all indebtedness is settled."

The Syzmoor Innehav added more rooms to the man's former home and converted it into a group home for displaced families. The lady of the house cared for her three children, her adopted three children, and as many as six other displaced families needing assistance while they rebuilt lives disrupted by tragedy.

Andrew called his family together in May 1871. His children, his sisters and their families, and his attorney came to the family meeting. "First I must thank you all for answering my rather unusual request," Andrew began with his wife at his side, "but Kristina and I have come to a very difficult decision and I, that is we, need your consent." Kathryn and Angela shuffled uneasily in their chairs. "It is good that you show some uneasiness sisters for our decision could directly affect your operation of The Westmend Innehav and its charities. We are going to dissolve The Syzmoor Innehav. I do not have the energy our grandfather had and this enterprise is exhausting me. I have talked with Abram and he would like to keep some of the holdings to manage himself. He has agreed to continue to make payments to the Westmend Trust according to terms of cooperation between the Westmend and Syzmoor Innehav. However, I do not foresee that this will be required for one-third of all settlements from the sale of holdings will be immediately transferred into the Westmend Trust. I do ask that Westmend take over the group home that has plagued me since I first discovered that fire years ago. It is operating smoothly now but does need a firm hand on its resources."

"What will you do?" Kathryn, his youngest sister asked.

"I greatly enjoy my reindeer farm and we will keep the Katril mill." Andrew then smiled at his two daughters and laughed, "And I am told we have more grandchildren on the way. I might just take time to be a grandfather."

Caribou, or reindeer, were a large part of Andrew's life. The moment he first stroked a wild bull, at the age of four. At that moment a passion for reindeer was born within him. A passion which continued to grow throughout his adult life. When he brought the first caribou to the manor he built a pen to keep them. These few caribou grew into a herd of reindeer. Under advice from Vartesian, Nicholas' Chief Reindeer Herdsman from Alapouella Pohjantähti, Andrew moved the pen to a more suitable site with more space where his herds could grow. He took great pleasure visiting with the Sami, when he could find them, always learning something of value. Residents of the region could not understand why Andrew spent so much time and money breeding reindeer when they, caribou, were so plentiful in the wild and Sami sold reindeer at reasonable prices. Andrew would smile contentedly and invite visitors to his reindeer farm. Guests were always amazed at the consistent health and quality of his animals. Many visitors tried to purchase the uncommon white reindeer, but Andrew never sold them.

It took over two years to dissolve the Syzmoor Innehav down to the one mill in Katril. Gunther Hansen's two sons purchased the reindeer farm they had managed for many years, and most of the northern lands which they maintained as a preserve. Peder Anders, Kristina's brother, purchased the lodge and made it an inn. The manager of the northern mill, at Bradsvald, purchased timber rights and the mill, scaling back the operation. Abram made arrangements with tenants of the many residential holdings, or found investors willing to continue practices established by Jonathon Syzmoor. Six small businesses which had been rescued by the Syzmoor Innehav were transferred to Grieg Holdings, the new company owned and managed by Abram Grieg.

Unburdened from the responsibilities of the Syzmoor Innehav, Andrew found a new pleasure in serving as *The Woodsman*. Kristina returned to her seat beside Andrew on midnight runs which filled two or three nights a week. It was not uncommon for the couple to take help to locations beyond a night's ride, lodging in a friend's home. Both Andrew and Kristina wore white hooded capes and stories of the ghostly woodsman with his bride were told in taverns and at dinner tables throughout central and northern Sweden. Pulled by two pure white reindeer, the sleigh flew through the air leaving a cloud of snow and ice behind it. It never left any tracks or evidence that it was truly where it had been seen. Nicholas had told Jonathon that the magical sleigh could be used without snow, however he had never tried. Andrew not only tried but used the sleigh on every Woodsman's journey throughout the year; a sight which increased rumors and legends of the mystical Woodsman.

Kristina only occasionally accompanied Andrew on visits to Alapouella Pohjantähti when their children were young, even though Natasha invited her. After Andrew retired, Nicholas was under strict orders to never bring Andrew without Kristina. The two wives had become fast friends, enjoying each others' company while their husbands did whatever it was they did.

On August 22, 1887, Kristina and Andrew were resting in the gardens behind their manor when Kristina asked, "Andrew, how many families has *The Woodsman* served?"

"Do you mean since we became *The Woodsman* or since Grandfather began his midnight rides?"

"Well, both."

"We could figure it out by simple math. Grandfather rode about three times a week for nineteen years. I suppose we have continued the same number of visits and we have been riding for nearly thirty-seven years since Grandfather died. So that would be fifty-five years or nearly eight thousand six hundred nights."

"But we rarely visit only one family in a night, we must average two or three families each night," Kristina added.

"Yes, that is a lot of families over a lot of years. Why would you ask?" Andrew looked at Kristina, puzzled by their discussion. "You look a bit pale, are you okay?"

"Just a bit of indigestion. Would you get me a small glass of sherry, please?"

Andrew stood and kissed his wife gently, "I will be right back."

Andrew returned with two glasses of sherry, however Kristina was not able to share hers with him. Her eyes were closed and she still had a trace of Andrew's last kiss on her lips, but her heart had stopped. Andrew sat with his wife, holding her hand while tears rolled softly down his cheeks.

Andrew and Kristina met when they were only four years old, married at the age of nineteen, and celebrated forty wonder-filled years of marriage. More than one-hundred-fifty guests filled the village square in Katril to celebrate Kristina's life with their three children and her three siblings. At the end of the funeral Nicholas walked over to Andrew and taking his arm told him, "Come ride with me."

Nicholas took Andrew to a home in need of help. "I took the liberty of picking up what was needed before Kristina's funeral. Won't you help me please?"

Moving slowly, Andrew picked up a parcel of meat and stumbled toward the cabin. Inside it was very humble and clean. The wood bin contained two pieces of wood and the larder was low but not empty. "Cut that meat, won't you?" Nicholas asked as he silently reviewed the memorabilia around the cottage. When Andrew finished cutting the meat Nicholas called to him again, "There are two more parcels in the sleigh; would you get them, please." Andrew did as he was asked, finding a bag of potatoes and a bundle of wood. Bewildered, Andrew took the parcels to the cottage where Nicholas pointed to the larder and wood bin. Nicholas then signaled Andrew to leave. Walking to their sleigh, Nicholas reached into his cape and pulled out a dog treat. Smiling, he tossed the chewy treat to a dog that had been sleeping around the corner of the cottage.

"What was that about?" Andrew asked as Nicholas

snapped the reins of his sleigh.

"They have family visiting for Kristina's funeral. You have helped many members of this family."

"That cottage was not in need of supplies," Andrew challenged. "I feel certain they had a side of meat hidden safely away."

"Maybe," Nicholas smiled. "Tell me, how do you feel?"

"Better, I think."

When they reached The Manor, Natasha came out to greet them. "Step aboard, my bride," Nicholas called to his wife. "Andrew, rest for a few days. I will be sending you some distant names soon, maybe Abram can ride with you." In the blink of an eye Nicholas and Natasha were gone.

Andrew continued serving as *The Woodsman* for many years, often with Abram at his side. Without the love and energy of Kristina, Andrew's own energy faded. His interest in business languished and while still a valued member of the community, he only repeated his acts of generosity and kindness. His heart was gone.

III
Abram Grieg
1866 - 1890
Born December 23, 1846, Katril, Sweden
Died February 21, 1890

Abram kept multiple diaries and journals. His story is told through excerpts from his own record.

13 October 1854, Friday
I suppose I should begin this journal by introducing myself. I am Abram Grieg. On this date I am eight years old. I was born on Mid-Winter's Eve of the year 1846. My father is *The Woodsman*, a friend and companion of Nicholas, that is Saint Nicholas. I plan to keep a journal of my trips and adventures with my father, *The Woodsman*, and someday to log my own travels when I become the next *Woodsman*. I believe this is an honorable ambition, to serve those who are less fortunate. My father inherited this role from his grandfather, Jonathon Syzmoor. I will now tell of my first trip with *The Woodsman*.

I met Father at the door as he was leaving for his journey. He told me I could tell no one of our trips. Our activities had to be secret. I agreed. Who would believe that I journeyed with *The Woodsman*? Our first stop was at the house of a wood carver. I cannot include his name because of my oath of secrecy. I have seen this man's carvings, so I believe he has a very giving heart. I told my father so. His cottage was humble but reflected his heart's faith and generosity.

While the first cottage showed me a very generous heart, our second stop was very different. It was filthy. I took care of the fire, as *The Woodsman* instructed, but I have never been so glad to leave a place. Father explained to me that we are servants and should not judge a family by what we see. I find this difficult.

19 January 1855, Friday

Today our journey included cottages of two families. They are some distance apart but still within the region of Katril. I reminded myself at the start that I should not judge for I am a servant of Nicholas, who judges no one. My task is to carry firewood. My arms were loaded with wood for the fire as we entered the first cottage. After seeing to the meager flame, I looked around to see what was important to the family. *The Woodsman* has told me to do this at every visit. I was alarmed when I recognized the boy sleeping on the cot in the corner. Looking to the loft I saw a hand hanging down and realized that it was his sister's hand. He has four sisters who sleep in the loft, two older than he. Even though I know this boy I have never spent any time with him. Yet, standing in his cottage with Father's staff lighting everything in its soft glow, I was intrigued. I have never visited a cottage in secret where I personally knew someone of the family. While I cannot say that I found anything revealing, just being there felt awkward and puzzling. I cannot think of any other family we have visited where I have had this feeling. I did not know the second family we visited tonight and felt no undo emotion when we left. Silently serving someone you know is both confusing and rewarding.

1 March 1855, Thursday

This is not the account of anything that has happened today but the journal of my trip with Father on 16 February, Friday. I am now able to record my thoughts from that night.

Our first three visits occurred without incident. At our final stop of the night I carried an armload of wood to the cottage, but being exhausted by the long night I dropped a number of pieces before entering. After quietly placing what I carried in the bin beside the fireplace, I ran out to pick up what I had dropped. With four pieces of wood in my arms, I turned back to the cottage but was stopped by a very large dog. Standing at the doorway was a black mastiff, standing over a meter at the shoulders and weighing at least fifty kilograms. I could see drool dripping from his snarling mouth. Nicholas had instructed me to make eye contact with animals that challenge me and they will not charge. I looked the beast squarely in his eyes. Father had given me dog treats for just such a time as this, but when I looked down to see what I had pulled from my pocket, I broke eye contact. Before I could pitch the treats to the dog, he was on me; grabbing my arm in his mouth. His jaws were powerful and I remember that his breath was just as bad, probably from eating wild animals in the forest. Father came to my aid, beating the dog with his stick. I remember trees and stars flashing past, but my next clear memory was Doctor Smalz examining my arm at our manor. I do not like dogs of any size.

25 December 1855, Christmas Day
The pain in my arm returned today. It has healed, physically, but when I saw Nicholas at our annual celebration, I felt - I was ashamed and my arm began to ache. I immediately ran to my room and wrapped my arm in a blanket.

25 December 1856, Christmas Day
Nicholas arrived for our open house in very good spirits. He brought his wife, Natasha, with him. She is a very friendly lady. She helped me talk with Nicholas about my problem. She told me that Nicholas and my father had talked about my event with the dog. I admit that even after talking with this charming lady, I was still nervous about approaching Nicholas. As I walked up to him, he set me at ease by wishing me happy birthday. Today is my tenth birthday. I could tell he was sincere when he invited me out to the rear patio for a conversation. I will write his words, as I remember them.

"*Your father tells me, young squire, that you are troubled about carrying his staff when he is ready to hand it down.*"

I watched him without speaking and silently nodded my head. I believe I must have looked down at the ground because I remember his hand lifting my chin as he squatted down next to me.

"*Do you see those stars?*" Nicholas pointed toward a clear sky filled uncountable sparkling lights. "*To our eyes all the stars look alike, yet every one is different. If you select a few stars and study them for many nights you will see what I mean."*

I looked at the countless stars that filled the sky and wondered how he could see any differences between any of these tiny points of light.

"As each of those stars is different, so is the service each of us yields to our fellow man. Your father does not serve as his grandfather did. I cannot serve the way your father does. So, when it comes your time to serve, your service will be different as well. Do not dwell on what you are unable to do. Instead, draw strength from what you can do."

I looked into this old man's eyes and saw a wisdom there I had never seen before, probably because he had never talked with me as a man before now.

"I do wish to serve, to walk in my father's path," I told Nicholas with as much confidence as I could find.

"You will, young squire, you will," Nicholas assured me with a smile. *"But you have many years to discover your strengths. Do not worry about the past, for it is gone. Feast your eyes on your future for I believe we shall have a rich friendship."*

The rest of the evening went well, except for when Mother and Father embarrassed me with their announcement of my birthday. I much prefer the quiet acknowledgment of Nicholas and his words of encouragement. But I doubt that I will ever be able to get rid of my fears.

17 February 1860, Friday

I cut myself badly today using the knife Father gave me for my birthday. I have been learning about carving wood, using soft wood, and am getting to be quite good. I admire those people who can produce a work of art from an ordinary piece of wood and find it relaxing and enjoyable to carve. But today I tried a piece of oak and found it much more difficult to manage. My blade slipped as I attempted to remove a large piece of wood from today's carving and the blade sliced across my thumb. Martha is good at bandaging cuts such as this because her husband, Jensen, uses his knives wildly while cooking. She said I will have a nice scar but will heal. It will be a week or longer before I can hold the wood for carving again.

7 May 1864, Saturday

Final examinations are only weeks away, however my desire to study is hampered by the arrival of warmer spring weather. As this is my first year at Bronkton University, I wish to take full advantage of all the university has to offer. Weary of elementary business studies I took a break from studying this morning and strolled around the campus. Several of my classmates were laying about on blankets in the sunshine surrounded by their books. A few invited me to join them, but I see no point in pretending to study with so many distractions surrounding you. I will keep my books in my room. I also witnessed students, some I know to be very serious about their studies, deserting their books for the company of members of the opposite sex. Students of the nursing academy find the company of students of the professional arts very promising. One of these young ladies flattered me with her attentions for nearly a week, but today I saw her in the company of the son of a wealthy banker. I have no patience for this springtime ritual of courting and am very envious of the life Mother and Father have spent together. I wonder if they met as adults, would they have the same life they had meeting at the age of four years? When I returned to my room to study, my eyes were drawn to my journal of visits with *The Woodsman*, which I keep on the shelf above my desk. I did not pull it down for there is such a gap in its pages that it pains me, yet I do draw comfort knowing that Mother is accompanying *The Woodsman* once again.

27 April 1866, Friday

As I walked back to my dormitory to resume my studies this morning I was met by a most welcome friend. Nicholas. Thinking back on our meeting I find it strange that not one of my classmates stopped or even acknowledged that I was speaking with this distinguished gentleman. One might almost believe that they did not even see that he was there. Something to puzzle.

Nicholas had come to ask my assistance in enrolling a student at the university. He had recently received a correspondence from a family seeking his assistance in the matter of enrolling their eldest son. Eager to be of assistance, I immediately took my friend to the Dean of Admissions, Mister Thomas Eklund. I was eager to watch the interaction of these two gentlemen for I knew Mister Eklund to be very strict in his business practices. Once I made the introductions, the two men talked with one another as old friends. The only thing missing was a tankard of ale in each of the men's hands.

I have studied interactions of people in all classes of work these past three years at the university, yet I feel I learned more watching Nicholas in this brief encounter than in all my years of observation. Mister Eklund did admit the young man, provisionally, and Nicholas set up a trust account to cover his expenses.

7 September 1866, Friday

I have been quite nervous about returning to nighttime outings with my father and have allowed this nervousness to delay my stepping forward to join him. I recognized the signs of father preparing to go out after supper - checking the meat locker, gathering blankets, counting bundles of wood, talking with Star and Glimmer (his reindeer companions). When it came time to load the sleigh, I picked up three bundles in the kitchen. "Are you riding with me tonight?" Father asked. I simply smiled and carried the bundles to the sleigh. I could feel my heart racing and my breath was short, difficult to take in. I stroked Star's head, waiting for Father to come out. I waited for Father to step into the sleigh before I sat next to him, not looking at him but looking straight ahead. My heart was racing so hard I felt as though I was going to lose consciousness. My incident with the dog was eleven years ago, yet it haunts me as though it were just yesterday. In all my studies at university I could find no true justification for this specter, yet it persists.

It seemed an eternity before we reached the first house. As father stopped the sleigh about fifty feet from the cottage, I searched the woods and cottage for signs of animals. "There are no dogs tonight," Father offered with a smile. I smiled back and turned to my old task of carrying wood. Father directed me to grab a blanket as well. Before repairing the fire I tried to cast my eyes around the cottage, as I had been instructed years before. I was having such difficulty breathing that I quickly put the blanket on the table and released the bundle of wood into the bin beside the fireplace. Reaching for the first piece of wood to stoke the dying fire, nearly gasping for air, I had to drop it and exit the cottage. Once in the fresh air my dizziness faded, my breathing relaxed, and I could feel my heart slow. "What am I doing here?" I thought, but the second and third visits were much easier. With each visit I became less apprehensive and more functional. I was even able to cast my eyes about the third cottage and discovered it to be the home of a childhood friend, now grown with a child of his own.

20 November 1866, Wednesday
Father has put me to work at the mill, learning the process of The Syzmoor Innehav just as he did, one unclean task at a time. When I ride with *The Woodsman*, I frequently experience problems with breathing as we approach the cottages. I attribute this to a simple fear of animal attack, dogs specifically, and trust that Father will not take me where large dogs are present. My apprehensions have been so powerful at times that I cannot even set foot into the sleigh at the manor, waving Father off to travel alone.

This evening I was in good spirits as Father prepared to leave and loaded the sleigh without discussing the visits with him. The reindeer were harnessed and I was waiting in the sleigh when Father came out and sat down. Lifting the reigns, he paused and looked at me, "One of our visits has a dog." I felt my body go cold and my arm, the one ripped by the dog one hundred twenty-nine months ago, eleven and a half years, pained me as though the dog's teeth were sinking into my flesh at that moment. I wanted to go! I MUST overcome this fear, but tonight was not my night to be a hero to my own trepidation. I stepped from the sleigh and watched *The Woodsman* ride off into the night.

25 December 1866, Tuesday

Father, *The Woodsman*, left early last night to complete the list Nicholas had given him at mid-Winter Festival. I do not know if there were dogs at any of the homes. Father did not invite me. Unable to sleep, I went to Father's office and poured a glass of sherry. I believe I might have been waiting for him, however I truly am not sure. As I stared into the glowing embers in the fireplace, I felt a hand on my shoulder. Expecting to see Father, I turned and beheld a most unusual sight. Nicholas was there, yet he was not there. I could see him yet I could not see him. He handed me a slip of paper on which were written the words "Go to my sleigh and wait." I did as instructed.

When I reached the sleigh, it was not entirely there. The sleigh and two men shimmered, as ghostly images. Reluctant to step onto the image I placed my hand on the side. As I waited the shimmering stabilized, that is it became solid. Suddenly Nicholas stood beside me, appearing as normal. I stepped into the sleigh and rode with this man of Christmas and his assistants as we delivered gifts to many homes throughout Scandinavia and other regions along a corridor to the south.

After several stops I began going into homes with Nicholas and I observed how he not only left gifts but admired the little things which made each home unique. He had instructed me to do this on my *Woodsman* visits, but it was inspirational to see the teacher doing as he instructed. I felt Nicholas grow agitated with me a number of times as I took time to really examine some articles on visits, slowing his progress somewhat. His two assistants, Vartesian and Dorf, began prodding me to keep on their timetable.

I felt hours pass as we visited countless homes, yet as I looked at the many clocks very little time passed. Nicholas answered my concern about this as "It is one of the mysteries of Christmas." We worked our way with incredible speed down to Cape Town, South Africa whereupon Nicholas looked at his watch and announced, "We have just enough time to get you home."

Traveling north on our return Nicholas asked me, "Abram, are you ready to resume visits as *The Woodsman*?"

"That is why I could not sleep tonight," I replied. "Father went out and did not ask me to join him. If I knew there were no dogs, I believe I could visit in the homes of those we can help. Quite honestly, I wonder if there is not a better way I can be of service."

Nothing else was said for we returned to the manor shortly after that. As I stepped from the sleigh, Nicholas looked at me with an uncharacteristically long face and said, "It was a pleasure to have your company. As soon as I am out of sight raise your hands over your head and clap once, solidly. You should also get something to eat before returning to bed."

"Returning to bed?" I thought. We had been up for hours, no days. I watched as the sleigh disappeared and pondered how this trip could have happened. Feeling fatigued, I did as Nicholas had instructed. I raised my hands over my head and clapped them together. There was a flash of light and a rumble of thunder. I suddenly felt exhausted. After a rather robust snack which I shared with Father when he arrived, I went to bed. The clock in Father's office read 1:43.

6 April 1868, Monday
Today marks a new era for The Syzmoor Innehav, for today we opened an office in Lansvardt. My great-grandfather, Jonathan Syzmoor, managed this vast enterprise from his study at the manor and my father continued this practice until today. I have, for many months, been discussing with my father the advantages of a commercial office in the village. He has finally relented. It will now be my primary function within The Syzmoor Innehav to manage our office, three office personnel, lease accounts, and accounts payable. Adam, who serves as father's legal counsel and who is married to Father's

sister, Angela, endorsed this idea suggesting that Angela be given a private office within our space to manage The Westmend Innehav. I have arranged this but fear that Aunt Kathryn will be a significant distraction when she visits with Angela. Her insatiable zest for life increases with her age.

I have also taken an apartment near the office. Father has always managed business from his study so it seemed prudent that I keep myself close to the center of operations.

Editor's note: the three Grieg siblings - Andrew, Angela and Kathryn - are the grandchildren and heirs of Jonathan Syzmoor and his business enterprises.

28 August 1868, Friday
Riding with Father has been rather difficult when I am staying in Lansvardt. To ease his and Mother's concerns, I have agreed to return to the manor each Saturday after we close the office. I will then be available to ride with and assist *The Woodsman* on Saturday outings. I do not wish to completely give up the quiet and solitude my apartment provides.

21 September 1869, Tuesday
While visiting the mill today, I picked up a small piece of wood. This piece was round, approximately four centimeters across and one half centimeter thick[3]. Turning the oak coin about in my fingers I became intrigued. Looking around where I found this piece, I found six more of similar size. I am most curious about how they will carve.

27 September 1869, Monday
The oak chips I found last week are wonderful to carve. With care and patience I can release images in a relief pattern on both faces of the wood. This activity is both relaxing and challenging. Today I asked Hans to cut three dozen pieces such as I found last week. Tomorrow I shall venture to a nearby furniture shop and get assistance finishing one of my coins. On one coin I have carved a wreath of holly and

---

[3] Dimensions of coin - about the size of an American Silver Eagle Dollar, one and one-half inches across by one fifth inch thick

evergreen wrapped together. Nicholas explained to me that life has both good and bad fortune, often both at the same time. I believe my wreath will convey this thought. As Father leaves his sticks with the beautifully etched bark as a token of his visit, I shall leave a coin. My challenge now is to find a design for the other side that will be of import to the task at hand.

21 June 1870, Summer Solstice

Nicholas came to me today with a most unusual request. He instructed me to open a bank account for a small orphanage in northern Finland. I find this request to be odd on two points. First, this region of Finland has no population to support or require an orphanage and second, I have witnessed him establishing a trust without requiring any assistance. When I challenged the wisdom of this action he replied, *"Do not worry about the location; this orphanage is needed. As for needing your assistance, I could easily do this myself but believe it would be better for you to do it for me. Just as your father visits families in need, I will ask you to see to special matters. Do you object to these tasks coming to you?"* I assured my dear friend that I would be glad to set up the trust and assist with any other tasks he should need my help with. To that end, as Nicholas has indicated that he will have special tasks for me, I will keep record of these tasks not in my daily journal but in a special book, to be set aside just for these requests.

Editor's note: entries from the journal of Nicholas' requests will be identified as "from the Woodsman's journal."

28 June through 29 July, 1870 - a compilation of dates from the Woodsman's journal

Nicholas asked me to visit an orphanage located in a remote community of Inari, Finland. I was wise enough to ask for directions, but what he told me was, *"Go to the lodge in Bradsvald, then follow your nose eastward until you get there. It is a small community at the southern end of Inarijärvi, a rather large lake some know as Lake Inari."* I must remember to commend

Nicholas on his accuracy, Lake Inari is the largest lake I have ever encountered. A full three days travel from Bradsvald with exceptional weather.

The orphanage is in reality an old monastery which was abandoned by the church due to being in such a remote location that civilization would most likely never arrive. In addition to the orphanage there is one church, a very small market, and about forty to fifty residents within twenty-five kilometers. The headmaster explained that their only need was a meager account to draw upon when they purchase supplies in Sodankylä, a larger village three days travel from Inari. At my request, Levi, the head master of the orphanage, agreed to travel with me to Sodankylä to establish accounts where he traded. It took him two days to prepare for the journey.

Once we arrived in Sodankylä, Levi introduced me to his merchants of choice. It is my firm belief that two of the five men were thieves and I refused to encourage trade with them. Levi and I searched Sodankylä and the surrounding area for a day and a half to replace the sources for goods he previously acquired from these scoundrels. We then interviewed three bankers and two attorneys to assist Levi. We both agreed on the attorney of choice, however I had to yield on the banker when the attorney recommended Levi's choice over mine. Nicholas had provided me with a significant deposit to establish the account. Both the attorney and banker were instructed to send statements to me at six month intervals that I might keep abreast of any potential problems or shortfalls in the account. I guaranteed to cover a reasonable overage should it occur.

During our return to Inari I talked with Levi at length about the orphanage. He explained to me that fifteen of the twenty children currently in residence were from Sami families. When children were orphaned and their parents were set to rest at Hautuumaasaari, the children were then left at the orphanage if a relative could not take them. Levi went on to explain that Hautuumaasaari, one of the islands of Inarijärvi, has served as a cemetery for the Sami people since ancient times. The other five children were left at the orphanage in the early hours of different Christmas Days. I spent several days visiting with the residents of this small village, admiring their artwork and dedication to life. I had only one Woodsman's coin in my pocket when I departed.

18 November 1870, Friday - from the Woodsman's journal
Today I was returning from one of Nicholas' special tasks and I happened to be near the edge of a forest as the sun set beyond it. What caught my eye was a single evergreen tree, standing resolutely apart from the others. I was reminded of a message from Father Stephen, "Each of us is but one of many, but when the sun sets and you go to sleep, thank God for your blessings and he will watch over you as though you are the most important person in the world. When you wake in the morning with the sunrise, ask God for strength and He will help you all day long." This solitary tree in front of the sun is the image I have been seeking to carve opposite the holly and evergreen wreath. The tree is our soul, standing alone, ready to receive, and ready to serve.

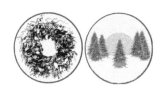

1 May 1871, Monday
I had the most unusual visit from Father today. He asked me what parts of The Syzmoor Innehav I considered most valuable. We talked about my answer for several minutes and he asked me what parts of the enterprise were the most volatile. Volatile? The nature of timber and land is a volatile mixture, but not such that it cannot be managed. He then pursued a discussion of the time it took to manage different aspects of Great-Grandfather's innehav as well as holdings Father had accumulated and now managed. After discussing the many facets of The Syzmoor Innehav, Father asked if I would assist him in dissolving the enterprise. He has given me

two weeks to select those parts I am interested in continuing to manage, under my own company, and to outline a release of the other holdings.

Editor's Note: Andrew met with his children and all concerned on May 21, 1871 to announce his plans to dissolve The Syzmoor Innehav. Many of the tenant properties and six small businesses which had been rescued by the Syzmoor Innehav were transferred to Grieg Holdings, owned and managed by Abram Grieg. A few smaller properties were transferred or sold without profit to resident community members.

15 March 1873, Saturday *The Ides of March* - from the Woodsman's journal

Nicholas came to me on Friday two weeks back and asked me to save a hospital, but added "if it needs saving." His last words put me on guard to the situation I might be entering. Seeing the concern on my face, Nicholas handed me a letter. The last line read, "If we cannot settle this account by March 14, it will be The Ides of March for this hospital." We both agreed the letter was a bit dramatic, still I left the next day for Barneveld, Norway.

Upon my arrival I was greeted with great hostility. The structure I found was of old stone and had a decaying roof. Five of the six chimneys were sufficiently blocked as to pose a fire hazard. It was far too cold inside to effectively treat the ill. As I walked through the facility, with my coat on, I realized that the majority of the patients were children. I was told that many of these children were from Amsterdam, where the orphanages and hospitals are beyond safe capacity.

Reminding myself that I was not there to save, nor take pity on the patients but to see to the possible rescue of the physical facility, I pushed onward to the administrator's office. The accounts were a shamble, rent on the building was long overdue, hence the condition of the building. Other accounts against the facility were being referred to the courts for collection.

I took it upon myself to visit the owner of the facility, a

stark business man, as well as with many of the creditors of the hospital. At the end of the day I walked the grounds to clear my mind of senseless administrative practices and to formulate a solution. Without a change in the administration of this facility I could do nothing to save it. Having made my decision, I turned back to the hospital building and found Nicholas waiting for me.

"Your heart was crying," Nicholas told me.

Indeed. I reviewed all that I had learned with Nicholas and he offered a solution that might work. He informed me of a man in Amsterdam who had experience running an orphanage-based hospital and wished to move to a quieter location. Standing amidst the trees I added to Nicholas' solution, "We should build an orphanage and get the children out of the hospital."

Nicholas left to recruit a business manager. I settled accounts with the land owner by purchasing the hospital facility and its adjoining property, using funds provided by Nicholas. Nicholas returned two days later with Mister Markom. Together the three of us established a trust to hold the deeds of the property and to settle all outstanding claims against the hospital.

The hospital administrator returned to the practice of medicine, where his true talents lay. Mister Markom began plans for construction of a suitable orphanage on the adjoining property. I promised to visit quarterly as long as my assistance was required. On this day, the Ides of March, I reflect on the death of a conqueror and the birth of a promise supported by the love and generosity of a great man.

19 December 1883, Wednesday - from the Woodsman's journal

This entry is made as a reflection of the week just past, for I took my personal diary by mistake on an errand for Nicholas instead of this journal. My good friend stopped by my office Tuesday of last week and informed me that his lost spectacles had been located and needed to be retrieved. When I inquired as to where they had been lost he said, and I quote as best I can remember, "*I am not sure, but I believe that rascal Rolfh knocked my spectacles and my Christmas watch from my pocket when your father and I freed him from a bush.*" I had to laugh for Rolfh is a reindeer of exceptional personality.

I departed on Thursday for Kannus, a growing village in central Finland. I used this journey as an opportunity to relax and enjoy the brief glimpses of strong daylight. Most of my trip was spent in extended dawn or dusk conditions.

Arriving in Kannus on Sunday morning, I went to the church where I was told I would find the missing spectacles. Indeed, as I sat in a pew near the rear of the small church, the young minister, Christopher Brok, was slipping the spectacles on as he surveyed his congregation. His message was inspiring and very appropriate to the theme of the Joy of the third Sunday in Advent. Following the service I waited in the pew until the church had cleared. As I introduced myself to Reverend Brok he slipped the spectacles on, instantly realizing why I had come. These uncommon spectacles appeared scratched to most, however a gifted few are able to use them to see what is in the hearts of those before them. Reverend Brok had learned to use them well. While we talked, I considered leaving the spectacles in his charge, but my fear of the wrong person finding them pushed me on to my purpose. Almost as an after thought I inquired about Nicholas' Christmas timepiece. Reverend Brok chuckled and led me to his brother's house.

Immediately upon entering the humble home of Nils Brok, I spied the missing timepiece on the fireplace mantle. After a brief visit I retrieved the watch and rewarded Nils with a Woodsman's coin. He looked at it curiously as I looked carefully at Reverend Brok. Rather than giving the reverend a similar coin, I charged him and Nils with exploring the significance of my coin together, as brothers.

Editor's note: Abram returned to the church in Kannus two times, in June 1884 and again on 20 December 1885, the Sunday before Christmas. The Woodsman comments that Reverend Brok stumbled in his message only slightly and doubts that any of his congregation noticed. During his second visit he spent time with the children of the church and as a lesson for them explained the meaning of the engravings on The Woodsman's Coin, giving each child one of these special, hand carved coins to keep with their own personal treasures.

1 January 1886, Friday - from the Woodsman's journal
Nicholas stopped by today, but not with greetings for the new year. Indeed, he did not even seem to recognize that it was the first day of the new year. His purpose was to send me on a hunt. While making deliveries last week, on Christmas Day, the dear man lost his hat. He does not care about the hat itself but the pin in the hat was a gift from my great-grandfather, Jonathon Syzmoor, and is very important to him.

According to Nicholas I should first try the Church of Santa Maria la Mayor on the Plaza of Angels in Baena, Spain, the province of Cordoba. He recalls stopping for prayer with Father Miguel. If not found there, I should try a small farmhouse on the outskirts of Cabra, Spain where he was startled by the unexpected arrival of a large dog.

My first concern with this hunt was that I do not speak Spanish fluently nor have I ever been to this region of Spain. I know nothing of these people nor their culture. This could be quite an adventure with problems I would have to overcome when presented. Concerns about a large dog nearly forced me to decline this assignment, however believing all visits would be done in daylight I reluctantly accepted.

My journey to the south of Spain took eleven days, traveling by coach, train, and pony cart. It should have taken only eight days, however I missed two connections and had to wait for the next train going south. Being quite fatigued on arriving at Baena, Spain I secured lodging and rested before going to see Father Miguel.

I found the elderly priest in a garden which separated his home from the sanctuary of the Church of Santa Maria. He was in prayer and his dedication inspired me in a way I do not quite understand at this time. I look forward to talking with Father Stephen (in Katril) about this. When he concluded his prayers I approached him and explained why I was there. To my surprise he understood me. I spoke with broken Spanish yet he understood me. I shall do my best to recount our conversation for it was most pleasing.

"*I knew he was with me that night,*" Father Miguel smiled.

"*What do you mean?*" I asked.

"*I have always spent the first hour of Christmas Day in prayer,*" Father Miguel explained. "*Often during this blessed hour I feel the presence of a guiding spirit. Now I know the Bishop of Myra is praying with ME!*"

"*Did you find his hat where you prayed?*" I asked.

"*No, I am sorry I did not.*"

Father Miguel and I talked about Nicholas until late in the afternoon. He was a delightful host and left me feeling both filled with awe and a strange yearning as well.

Early the next morning I journeyed to Cabra. A journey made more difficult due to my poor grasp of the local language and trouble reading signs. Once I did find the village, I went to the center of town and traveled northwest as Nicholas had instructed. It is amazing to me how this man thinks I can travel by cart as simply as he does in his magnificent sleigh. Oh, the problems of roads! It was getting late when I finally found a farm such as Nicholas had described. As I approached the farm house, a large dog charged my pony cart, followed by a boy of about five years wearing Nicholas' hat.

Seeing the boy had some command over the beast, I nervously proceeded to inquire about Nicholas' hat. Using my best broken Spanish, I asked to see the hat. The boy screamed something I interpreted to be "MY HAT!" and went running inside, leaving the large dog guarding me. My heart raced and I began to sweat profusely as the beast continued his barking and jumping at my cart. It would have been easier had I been actually frozen by my fear, but I was seized by absolute terror actively seeking a way out. Not once did I consider that I was holding the reins to the pony in my hands ever so tightly and could simply ride out of the yard.

Some minutes passed before a beautiful young woman emerged from the house and secured the dog to a tree some distance away. Her face and generous actions showed deep concern for my state of mind as she brought me water. It was several minutes before I was able to speak and reveal the reason for my presence. The woman explained that the boy, Esteban, found the hat below Mother Mary and he believed it to be a special gift from the Christ Child.

I asked, as best I could, to simply examine the hat. The young mother smiled at the boy and nodded in my direction. Esteban offered the hat to me where I sat, still in the cart. Examining the hat I found the pin was not there and asked what had happened to it.

Esteban explained that there was no pin, whereupon I asked to see the location where he had found the hat. The mother took me into her small home and knelt in front of the statue of Mother Mary, just to the right of the fireplace. I looked around and caught a glint of something between the wood pile and the wall. Reaching behind the wood, I retrieved the lost pin.

Relieved that I had completed my quest I thanked the family and began to leave, however the woman insisted that I stay for supper as their special guest. I enjoyed their marvelous hospitality, far exceeding what I could expect from a family of their means. They asked me to spend the night but concerned for the dog's safety, he was still tied to the tree, I left and took a room at a local hacienda; Nicholas' pin in my vest pocket.

I returned the pin two weeks after I found it. In my years of knowing and working with Nicholas, I have seen many expressions on his face from extreme sadness to extreme joy, yet never before had I seen the expression of total relief. His dear friend had returned.

24 August 1887, Wednesday
Mother has died. This past Monday night. I returned home

this evening from a trip to the tenant properties, and found a great many people milling about the yard, the stables, and inside. Immediately I went to Father's study where I found my two sisters talking with Father Stephen. They were completing arrangements for Mother's memorial service, to be at noon tomorrow. Moments later Father walked in with Nicholas; they were making plans for *The Woodsman*. At that moment I felt empty and alone for the first time. Marianne has Thom and their four children, Hannah has Mark and their three daughters. Father has Nicholas. I am solitary by choice, but tonight, tonight my solitude is like an icy shroud and I truly feel alone.

19 June 1889, Wednesday

Today I had the great pleasure of taking August, a ward of Nicholas, to the VonBroten Medical School, an affiliate of my alma mater, Bronkton University. I met Nicholas and August in the village and showed August the important buildings and sites of the two schools as we walked to our appointment. Nicholas excused himself for another errand.

To my dismay I found our appointment was with Mister Mikol VonShiere. The same man who had been a constant annoyance as a bookkeeper during my years as a student at the University. This disagreeable man with a squeaky voice began our interview by telling us there were no openings in the Medical School and the only reason he was meeting with us was because the interview had been scheduled by Mister Eklund, president of the university. At the mention of Mister Eklund's name, my mind was filled with pleasurable memories as he was one of my favorite professors and a most influential personal advisor.

Throughout the interview Mister VonShiere's demeanor was cold and uncompromising. He challenged every answer that young August provided and threatened to have us thrown off campus when August explained that he was from Alapouella Pohjantähti. Mister VonShiere knew legends of this village and challenged its very existence. It was not until Mister Eklund and Nicholas dropped by that the interview progressed with propriety. Young August was granted provisional admission beginning with the next semester of studies.

23 February 1890, Sunday
I, Nicholas, close this diary for my dear friend and colleague Abram Grieg. He surpassed all of my expectations, as did his father, Andrew, and Andrew's grandfather, Jonathon. Each of these great men served their wide spread communities with unmatched love and devotion, rarely questioning my requests and always fulfilling them. I shall miss them, each of them, for they are indeed great men.

The End of the Journals of Abram Grieg

Editor's Comment:
> Abram was true to Nicholas' instructions to look around every cottage he entered. Whether he was there as The Woodsman or an invited guest, Abram looked for special features of every place he visited, so he might find a way to help his host. He became very good at spotting personal talents in wood craft, carvings, paintings, ceramics, carpentry and even metal work. He drew intense pleasure in finding someone with unusual needs and matching them with someone who had the talent to meet those needs. The following story, from the spoken legends of The Woodsmen, illustrates Abram's special gifts.

Nathaniel's Stars

Nathaniel rolled over and looked across the one room cabin. Sarah and Cynthia, his younger sisters, were sleeping near his feet. His mother and father huddled under a worn blanket beneath the small loft where his older brothers, Bret and Robert, slept. There was no flicker in the fireplace, the last piece of wood burned long ago. Cynthia's teeth chattered a bit and she was quiet once again.

Quietly, Nathaniel slipped to the floor and pulled his boot liners on. His big toe poked through on the left liner and his little toe tried to escape on the right. He would have to ask Father to make him a new pair with the next deer kill. Slowly Nathaniel opened the door, pausing for a few seconds to peer outside. He went into the quiet night.

Without intent the young man pushed through the snow to a spot about 35 feet from the door of his cottage. A cloud floated across the bright moon, casting a dark shadow and obscuring the cottage. Standing motionless, Nathaniel listened to the quiet of the night. There were no owls, no wolves, no sounds at all, not even the wind. Then he heard a sound that could not be heard in the daylight. The sounds of reindeer breathing hard. He heard their feet pounding through the snow. Turning around he heard a sleigh and saw them emerging from the dark.

Nathaniel's young eyes fixed on two large white reindeer,

side by side in harness. They appeared to be gigantic animals, their shoulders as tall as Nathaniel himself with their huge feet pounding through the snow. Their heads bobbing only slightly, their breath was so heavy it seemed to hang in the air before dropping under their feet as if frozen. There was a slap of leather urging the deer to pull on, then a powerful "WHOA, BOYS." The reindeer stopped in front of Nathaniel, who reached out and stroked the nose of the deer to his right. A large man, wearing a heavy green cape and furs of many kinds stepped out of the sleigh and walked to Nathaniel.

"If you don't scratch Patch the same as you are scratching Biston, he will knock you over."

Nathaniel stared at the large man with suspicion. As the boy raised his left arm, the second reindeer pushed him with his head. Nathaniel chuckled and rubbed the deer's nose.

"Told you he was the jealous type. What is a young man such as yourself doing in the middle of the road on a night cold as this? And without a cape or coat?"

Nathaniel looked into the eyes of the man. The cloud had just cleared the moon and midnight light filled the man's eyes with stars. Removing his fur-lined hood, the man's smile warmed and reassured Nathaniel that this man could be trusted. "Couldn't sleep . . . thought I would come out and look at the stars . . . listen to the night," the young boy replied.

"I suppose that is your home," the man gestured back to Nathaniel's cottage. "Don't see any smoke on your chimney."

"No, ran out of wood. We aren't allowed to cut the trees in these woods. Have to go to the timber station and we don't have any way to get there. Last time they found wood we cut ourselves we had to walk to the station and buy our own wood back. Father was not very happy about that."

"Well, I have a few pieces of good hardwood in my sleigh. If you will help me, I might be able to get your fire going." The man removed his glove and put out his hand, Nathaniel took the offer and followed the man to his sleigh.

This sleigh seemed almost magical. It was low to the ground, dark green in colour with bronze trim. There were carvings of deer, bear, birds and a large forest all around the sides. It was big enough to carry Nathaniel's entire family, yet had only one bench for sitting. Nathaniel climbed onto the seat and looked into the back of the sleigh. There was enough wood to warm his cottage for two, maybe three, days. There were also two other bundles wrapped in sailcloth. The man stood in front of Nathaniel and picked up the reins. With a quick snap he directed the reindeer and the sleigh to the cottage door. He pulled a small axe from under the seat and several logs from the back of the sleigh. Nathaniel opened the door to the cabin and led the man to the cold fireplace.

Without any direct intent to awaken the sleeping family, nor to be overly quiet, the man put the wood near the fire. With a heavy sigh he looked around the cottage, then split one of the logs into kindling. A wad of batting, flint, and steel appeared from his pocket and a fire blazed within minutes. After retrieving another two arm loads of wood, the man surveyed the cottage again, this time with purpose in mind.

"I see your supply of meat matches your supply of wood."

"Father plans to take Bret and Robert hunting as soon as he gets well. Bret and Robert aren't old enough to go out by themselves. They can get a deer if it comes nearby, but that doesn't happen much any more."

Without another comment the man returned to his sleigh and brought one of the bundles in. He unwrapped it and placed a side of pork and loaf of bread next to the fire to warm.

"You like to watch the stars?"

"Yes, they don't ask for anything and seem so constant. If you squint your eyes, you can see images in the stars . . . did you know that?"

The man chuckled and replied, "Yes, I have seen many images in the night sky. If I were to give you some stars to watch inside, would you settle back into your cot and get warm?"

"You can't bring stars inside."

Putting a finger to the side of his eye the man picked up his axe and went out into the night. Shortly he returned with a spindly tree branch. Again he went to his sleigh and returned with a spool of string and a bag. He secured the branch to a table leg and then produced several candles from the bag, which he secured to the branches. Retrieving a small stick from the fire he lit the candles. "Stars," he whispered with a smile. As he put the stick back into the fire, he noticed a collection of carved figures on the mantle. Carefully, the man picked up a reindeer and a bear.

"Who did these carvings?"

"Father is teaching me. I did the reindeer and Father did that bear. I have a bear I am working on over here." Nathaniel pulled a box from under his cot and retrieved a block beginning to resemble a bear.

"Since you carved this reindeer, what would it cost for me to have it?"

"You can have it . . . I have a box full of reindeer."

"Thank you. What is your name?"

"I am Nathaniel . . . who are you?"

"Most folks call me *The Woodsman* . . . but my friends call me Abram. I must go now. Thank you for the reindeer."

Nathaniel smiled and began to stare at the candles, his own personal stars. He barely heard the reindeer pull the sleigh away.

The next morning Nathaniel's family woke to a warm cabin and hot pork and bread ready to be eaten. Nathaniel explained they came from *The Woodsman*. "I thought that was a legend made up by folks across the river," Father laughed.

"Maybe, but this is the best tasting legend I have had in a long time," Bret replied.

Later, that same day as the sun began to slide past its height, there was a knock on the cottage door. Mother opened the door and found a man in a heavy fur cape, carrying a large wooden case. "I am here to see Nathaniel's father," the man stated as he politely pushed his way into the cottage.

Looking toward the fireplace he saw a side of pork, about one third eaten. The supply of fire wood was ample, but needed replenishing. Looking around he saw Bret and Robert, "You two, there is some wood in the back of my sleigh. Bring it in and store it properly. Now, Father, I understand you have been ill. I am a doctor, most of my patients receive treatment at my office in Lansvardt, however a mutual friend suggested I visit you here. Now, tell me what is wrong."

Father spoke hardly three words before the doctor pulled him to his feet and began examining him. This family had never had professional medical treatment, but they all got full examinations that afternoon. "You are all suffering severe congestion and malnutrition. Nathaniel, go look on the seat of my sleigh. There is a box of fruit; bring it in please. You are each to have one piece of fruit every day. No more and no less. There should be enough there to get you back on your feet. Bret, if you look in my sleigh you will find a sailcloth with a leg of venison - it is smoked and ready to eat, after you warm it. Spread it out over the coming days, it should be enough until you can go hunting again. And when you get the first deer, treat the hide carefully. You all need new foot wraps."

Without another word the doctor crossed over to the mantle and picked up the bear that rested there. "I understand you have some reindeer as well." Nathaniel produced his box of reindeer. The doctor picked through the box and pulled out five carvings. "Are there more bear?"

Father directed Robert to retrieve a box from the loft. The box was full of carved animals. Examining each one, the doctor pulled out three bears, another reindeer, and four foxes. "I am a businessman, not given to charity. While this visit was paid for before I got here, I am going to make you a proposition. I will check back on you in a few weeks and I will give you one half copper for every animal you carve that I think my brother can sell in his store. That means I owe you seven coppers, if you will pick one more animal out for me." While the doctor counted out seven copper coins, Nathaniel grabbed another bear from his father's box.

"These show very good work and much talent. I hope we can continue doing business. Cynthia, will you and Sarah take these wonderful animals to my sleigh?" The girls gathered up the carvings and carried them to the sleigh, their voices filled with laughter.

Turning to leave, the doctor addressed the family one more

time, "Father, you have a very nice family. Get off your backside and sit up. Your chest won't drain when you lie down all the time. Nathaniel, watch your stars inside, on your tree, but with care! Don't go outside in the middle of the night." He winked and then closed the door behind him.

The Grieg Family Legacy
A Family in Devoted Service

Editor's Note: Jonathon Syzmoor was the first of The Woodsmen of Saint Nicholas. He served the requests of his mentor faithfully and quietly for nineteen years. Andrew Grieg assumed his grandfather's role in business and as The Woodsman. He served faithfully and quietly for a lifetime. Andrew's son, Abram, assumed a different role as The Woodsman. Injured by a large dog while accompanying his father on a delivery at the age of nine, Abram saw to business needs of Nicholas and made visits to homes only when assured there were no dogs present. Abram carried the title of The Woodsman with his father, Andrew, until a tragedy ended their service to Saint Nicholas.

It had been a week of hard weather, heavy snowfall mixed with ice. Trees were bowed down with accumulation and many were falling under the strain of excessive weight. Andrew stepped into the kitchen at the manor and dropped into a chair. He was exhausted.

"I have been given five names," Andrew moaned. "I am not surprised, but I know I cannot do them all in a timely manner."

Pernilla, the cook, poured a cup of cider, adding a bit of brandy. Handing it to Andrew she replied, "We have the meat, but you do need help."

"I will help, Father," Abram agreed from the door.

"Thank you, there is no mention of any dogs or other concerns, just five families in despair," Andrew acknowledged. "We should schedule them for tomorrow night. I expect there will be more before this weather clears."

"I will be ready," Abram replied and left the kitchen.

The next day, Friday, February 21, 1890, was spent collecting clothes, blankets, meat, and other food needed for the five families. Andrew made sure there were enough "treats" for any dogs they might encounter.

The sleigh left the manor shortly after ten o'clock under a

dark sky with snow falling lightly. At the first stop Andrew and Abram established their order of work and all went smoothly. Stop number two occurred without a word being spoken. While en route to the third house, Abram asked his father, "How many years have you been serving as *The Woodsman*?"

"I began at the age of eighteen," Andrew replied. "And I am sixty-four now. You do the arithmetic."

"Forty-six years," Abram replied with awe. "That is more than twice what great-grandfather served."

"You say that like it is a sentence pending execution. It is a privilege to serve and it has kept me alive far past my peers, most of whom merely exist from day to day with little, if any, purpose. Grandfather did not begin until he was forty-three years old and he served until he died at the age of sixty-two. Our next stop is near."

Quietly the two *Woodsmen* set to work; Andrew carried meat. Abram managed blankets, wood, and other necessities. As they were leaving the cottage, a dog of moderate size, weighing about seventy kilograms, charged at them from under a bush. Andrew quickly stopped the charge with his staff and tossed a dog treat to the animal. The dog lost no time retrieving the ball of meat and meal, returning to his hiding place to work on the chewy delight.

Abram was visibly shaken by the event but regained his composure before they reached the fourth home. This home had four children and both parents; all children received clothes and blankets. Abram elected to rekindle the fire first, so he carried only a bundle of firewood on his first trip into the cottage. To their surprise there was a lantern burning softly on the table. Looking around, *The Woodsmen* saw three young children sleeping huddled together in one bed. Assuming the lantern was providing light for their comfort, it was left alone. With light from the lantern, Andrew did not need his staff which he placed next to the door where he could retrieve it as they finished.

Abram revived the fire, then returned to the sleigh for other essentials. After placing the clothes on the table, he and

Andrew began draping blankets over the sleeping occupants. The younger *Woodsman* smiled as he bent over to drape a blanket across a child sleeping alone. Without warning, without a sound, a large dog lunged from a dark corner near the child's bed, grabbing Abram at the shoulder and driving him backwards. Crashing into the table, Abram's head smashed through a low cabinet door. As the table shattered under the impact of Abram and the dog, the lantern spilled onto the clothes where its soft light exploded into flame, spreading across the floor in the straw and other debris covering the soil beneath. Andrew tried to reach his staff, but flames blocked his path. Turning, he grabbed the three children and burst through the flames into the frigid outdoors. The crashing awoke the parents who picked up the older child and followed Andrew.

As quickly as he put the children in the sleigh, Andrew turned back to the cottage. Now engulfed in flame, its heat scorched those standing by the sleigh, melting Andrew's entire sense of life. Three times he started back toward the cottage to rescue Abram, his son. Every attempt to reach the door was stopped by roaring flames, even setting fire to his own cloak. Unable to find a thought, Andrew stood, staring into the flames which dried his tears and scorched his face. Hearing cries from his sleigh, *The Woodsman* answered that call.

"I have some more blankets in the back. Wrap your children quickly," Andrew instructed as he loaded everyone into the cargo area of the sleigh. Without looking back, he raced to the chapel in Katril where the family could be cared for.

"I will take that," Nicholas called softly to a man looking at an unusual wooden staff lying in the doorway of a burned out cottage. Without hesitation the man handed the staff to Nicholas and returned to his gruesome task of sifting through the remains of a family home.

"Were there any human remains found?" Nicholas asked solemnly.

"A bit," the man replied. "They were collected and sent to the chapel. Do you know who it was?"

Nodding quietly, Nicholas returned to his sleigh and left.

Abram's funeral was attended by his two sisters, Hannah and Kristina, and their families, sixteen men and women from the village of Katril, three friends from Landsvardt, and his father who sat without moving or speaking.

Nicholas stood silently in a corner in the rear of the chapel holding the staff of *The Woodsman* respectfully. He approached Andrew after all had left the chapel. Before Nicholas could speak, Andrew raised his hand and whispered, "Keep it! Please inform Father Stephen and the others that *The Woodsman* has died."

Nicholas wrapped his arms around his friend. After some time Kristina touched her father's shoulder letting him know it was time. Reluctantly Nicholas released Andrew and watched him leave the chapel.

IV
Jameson Thorpe
1890 - unknown
Born May 19, 1863, Øvre Stjørdal, Norway

Jameson kept a personal diary telling of his days, records of sales and purchases, even family traditions and events he wanted to remember. His story is retold from these pages.

Introduction

Nicholas stood alone in the chapel in Katril. The memorial service for Abram Grieg had concluded and all members of the family Grieg had left. Standing in the vast quiet Nicholas fell to his knees, raised his head, and called out, "Father, I know this great injustice is not of Your hand. I have lost dear friends and companions. I seek only to do Your work in the communities of Your children. Send me now to the one who will carry this staff and continue Your work. Awaken the next Woodsman and bring us together."

Slowly Nicholas lowered his head and knelt silently for some time, until Father Stephen touched his shoulder. Rising to his feet Nicholas informed Father Stephen, "The Woodsman is no more. I will tell you if he returns." Holding the Woodsman's staff firmly in his left hand and his own in his right, Nicholas walked slowly from the chapel into the darkness.

Nicholas carried the Woodsman's staff with him wherever he traveled, occasionally lighting the candle beneath its stone. The soft glow reminded him of the goodness displayed by the three men who had carried it and assured him that someday another would as well. Every night the former bishop lifted his request to his Father for a new Woodsman.

On December 6, 1890, Nicholas attended the Feast of Saint Nicholas in Leirfjord, Norge (Norway). He often attended this festival as Saint Nicholas, sharing his faith and stories with the faithful community. As he finished his last story of the day, his eyes met those of a man who had just arrived at the festival. Smiling from his heart, Nicholas blessed the waiting cakes and sent the children, young and old, off to enjoy their pastries.

Jameson's Story

My journey was coming to an end. A late autumn storm caused many delays for I would not normally be traveling into the month of December. However, as fate would provide, it was indeed a fortunate delay. This trip was to the northern boundaries of Norge (Norway). While I had planned to go to Hammerfest, winter weather stopped me at Leirfjord. My small wagon was filled with many trolls and other folk art. I am certain that Voltik, my pony, would have refused to walk one more step had I added but one more piece.

Common to northern Norge, morning chased the storm of the previous evening away. Bright sunshine melted ice from the night before, warming the air and my spirits. I was traveling south along the coast and entered the village of Leirfjord. As I passed through town, I noticed a large gathering of people outside a church. Curious, I pulled on the reins, asking Voltik to take our cart to the gathering. It was a festival, very uncommon for this time of year. Having discovered many wonderful works of art at local festivals, I took time to explore. Walking through the booths, I found craftsmen selling jewelry and little trollkiens but nothing that caught me as truly unique. One family did offer a wonderful warm beverage, similar to hot cider, but with a very distinctive flavor. Next to this family's booth was a pastry chef with a splendid array of artistic sweet cakes unlike anything I had seen before. My mouth and my stomach yearned for a treat. When I tried to purchase one I was told they were not for sale and I would have to wait for Saint Nicholas to bless them.

When the proprietor said the name "Saint Nicholas," I remembered that today was indeed the Feast Day of Saint Nicholas, December 6, 1890. Just then I heard loud laughter and walked toward the revelry. To my delight I found an old storyteller dressed as Saint Nicholas. He was just beginning a story.

After finishing a most delightful tale, the old storyteller paused in silence, surveying the faces of his audience. His eyes met mine and he smiled with an intensity that told me I must talk with this man, but he continued speaking to the gathering. "That will be enough stories for now, for I see that there are some fresh, sweet, Saint Nicholas pastries across the way. Consider them blessed as a gift from the One who gives us all through the generosity of our wonderful pastry chef. I will be there shortly, so please save me one!"

Immediately the children, all ages, rushed over to the pastry booth, leaving me alone in the presence of this marvelous old storyteller. I walked over to congratulate the old man on a story well told. He extended his hand before I reached him.

"That was a marvelous story, sir," I complimented him. "And I must say that you are probably the most convincing Saint Nicholas I have ever seen."

"Thank you," he replied with a light chuckle. "I look forward to this day for it gives me a special opportunity to share my heart with so many. On this day even the oldest of us is young at heart and expectant of a great treat." He pointed toward the pastry table and turned me with his other arm, "Come, let us see if there are any left."

We walked together to find there were exactly two pastries remaining. The pastry chef handed them both to the storyteller saying, "Nicholas, a wonderful story. You have added a most special blessing to our festival."

I looked at the storyteller almost in disbelief. Was his name actually "Nicholas" or was the pastry chef just taken in by the characterization? "I have never heard about the 'Bethlehem Tree.'[4] Did you construct this story or did you learn it somewhere?"

Smiling warmly the old storyteller told me how he had

---

[4] The story of "The Bethlehem Christmas Tree" can be found on page 71 of "Finding Nicholas, secrets of santa revealed by his woodsmen" by E. Gale Buck (c) 2011 by the Silver Wreath Incorporated.

once seen the tree and learned the story of its magic. When I challenged the validity of such a legend he replied, "Every legend, whether it be of generals or trolls or Christmas Trees or old Saints . . . every legend has some foundation in fact." He smiled and his eyes sparkled. He then asked me, "Why are you in Leirfjord today?"

"I am on my way home to Namsskogan. I travel extensively collecting folk art and when I saw the festival I hoped to find a treasure. Little did I know the treasure would be in the form of an excellent storyteller." As we walked through the booths, I noticed that the storyteller walked with two staffs. "Why do you carry two staffs?" I asked, hoping for another story.

The storyteller looked at me with a smile, "This gnarly old stick is mine. I have carried it for decades. This other staff belonged to a very dear friend of mine. I am seeking someone who has the strength and insight to carry it for him, possibly make it their own."

He stared into my eyes and offered me the second staff. With some hesitation I wrapped my hand around it. As my grip tightened I began to see the old man as more than just a storyteller. At that moment I felt an energy radiating from Nicholas and I wanted to learn more about this unusual staff he had placed in my hand . . . in my life.

"I am staying at the inn just down the road. Perhaps we can have supper together and talk," Nicholas told me. He then walked away, leaving me with the staff and many questions.

Voltik raised his head as I approached. I could tell he was looking at the staff I was still carrying, but he relaxed when I took him by the bridle and walked with him rather than climbing into the cart. It was a short distance to the inn and I enjoyed the walk. The staff felt natural in my hand and to my step. When I inquired about a room, the inn keeper laughed and replied, "Young man, you are in luck. We have but one bed left, however you must share this room with Saint Nicholas."

"That will be okay, I have met the old man," I told the inn keeper and paid him for my lodging and stabling for Voltik. After getting Voltik settled and my cart put away for the night, I settled myself in front of a fire in the corner of the dining area. I had just gotten comfortable when Nicholas arrived, handing me a mug of hot cider.

"Tell me about yourself," my host said, settling into a chair next to mine.

"I am Jameson Thorpe and I have a wonderful wife, Kasandra, who is pregnant with our first child," I offered with a big smile.

"How long have you been married?"

"We were wed on Christmas Day, last year."

"What work do you do? I saw your cart is loaded with carved figures. Trolls!"

"Yes, I sell hand carved figures to distributors around the world. Actually I purchase the works from regional craftsmen and work with several distributors who sell them around Europe and in the United States. The people in America like Norwegian Trolls."

"Have you ever seen a Norwegian Troll in the forest?" Nicholas asked with a concerned look on his face.

"No," I replied, trying not to laugh. "I have seen paintings and many different likenesses in carvings. Why?"

"Real trolls are over two meters tall, some three meters, with long arms and powerful legs. They have a bad temper as well, which is why I always carry oatmeal treats when I travel through these forests." Nicholas took a long draught of cider and looked directly into my eyes.

"No, I have never seen a real Norwegian troll," I replied and drank what was left of my own cider.

"Hmm," Nicholas replied. "How did you get into the business of buying and selling hand-crafted art?"

"My grandfather was a wood carver. He created wonderful works but was never able to sell them. Local people do not purchase local art, but I have developed contacts who sell for me and I sell at some festivals. I even take requests for specific types of work on occasion."

Nicholas sat quietly looking at me, rather, looking into me. I felt as though he was examining my soul. After what seemed an eternity he stood, "Let's get something to eat. The innkeeper's wife makes a wonderful stew and her bread is even better!"

We settled at a table where I found the stew to be very good indeed, and the bread was excellent. Half way through my dinner I stopped and asked, "What is the story behind the staff?"

"How does it feel to your hand?" Nicholas asked, putting his spoon in the bowl.

"Very natural. I thought my pony was going to kick me when he saw it, but he relaxed when I walked beside him. I have never walked with a staff before but this one feels natural. The candle in the top is most unusual. I do not believe I have seen anything like it."

Nicholas proceeded to tell me the story of Jonathon Syzmoor, Andrew Grieg, and Abram Grieg. By the time he finished we had each consumed another bowl of stew, devoured a loaf of bread between us, and had laid down on our cots. "The question now is," Nicholas concluded, "are you willing to accept the staff and the responsibilities which go with it?"

"I am not in a position to take food, clothing, blankets, and firewood to people in need," I replied quickly.

"I would not expect you to. I would expect you to look into your heart and see what gifts you have which you can share. Like the other three, you are a man of business, but unlike the others you can see beauty and opportunity where others do not. You also travel extensively; this could help." Nicholas paused and looked at me, allowing everything to settle in my mind and on my heart. "Sleep on it and we will talk some more in the morning."

Nicholas was asleep and snoring before my mind could fully accept him and what he had put before me. As I pondered our discussion, my mind recalled images of Nicholas, the Bishop of Myra, which I had seen in the shops of art dealers. I had to accept the similarity in features, yet these were artistic interpretations of another's descriptions. My mind was trying to make sense of our conversation, yet a peace in my heart eased me into a very deep sleep. Even with an incredible symphony of snoring coming from the cot next to mine.

I awoke in the morning to an unusual feeling, partly contented, partly apprehensive beyond description. Nicholas was gone, as were all his belongings. I stuffed my own belongings back into my sack and went down to the dining room. Nicholas was sitting at a table with two steaming bowls of oatmeal, a side of smoked meat, and two mugs of hot chocolate.

"I would say I took the liberty of ordering breakfast for you, but this is all they offer. Sit." After I sat across the table, Nicholas continued his morning greeting, "How did you sleep?"

"I had a bit of trouble getting to sleep. I pondered what you told me and I am apprehensive."

"You were sleeping quite well this morning, however I am delighted to hear you are apprehensive. I would have been concerned if you were not. What is troubling you most?"

"I do not know," I replied and took a spoon full of oatmeal. "It is not that I do not know what is bothering me. What is bothering me is what I do not know. I do not know what I have to offer you."

"If you knew what you had to offer, would you offer it?"

"I believe I would."

"Good. You do not need to know. You must be willing to discover. Life is not an event, it is an adventure to be lived and savored and lived some more. If we knew what our day would bring, many of us would change our course and very possibly miss some of our grandest moments. If you will take this staff, I will visit with you and Kasandra and we will learn together how our new Woodsman will change the world where he lives. Will you? . . . Will you bear the staff?"

I tried to find the words to say I would consider what was being offered. Before I could say anything, the innkeeper's wife delivered a package to Nicholas. "If you have finished, I would like to give a bit of this treat to your pony. Then, I have an appointment with a rather tall friend north of here."

Grabbing a block of smoked meat from breakfast, my bag,

and the staff, I followed Nicholas out to the stable. He unwrapped a large block of cake and broke off a piece, handing it to Voltik, who devoured it instantly. "I must be off, I will visit you in Namsskogan, soon."

Laughing out loud I called to Nicholas as he walked away, "What is that cake you gave to Voltik?"

"Oatmeal Cookie!" Nicholas called out as he waved goodbye.

"He was very convincing," I explained to my wife, Kasandra, for the third time.

"It is a beautiful walking stick and the glow from the candle is mesmerizing," Kasandra replied softly. "When will I get to meet your Saint Nicholas? Should I plan to wait up on Christmas Eve?"

"I do not know. I am only half certain that our meeting truly took place. I know for certain I met a wonderful storyteller but the rest . . . I know, or I think I know, that I talked with this storyteller and he gave me his second walking stick. I have told you about our conversation, yet when I hear his words in my voice . . . well, they seem to lose their credibility. I do not know what to expect nor when we will see him again . . . or if we will ever see him again."

The more I thought about my encounter with the storyteller, the more I began to question what took place. He spoke of helping people in need, trolls, and discovering something new about myself, about my life. As each day passed, I pushed the conversation and its emerging responsibilities further to the back of my mind. That is, until Christmas morning.

Kasandra and I woke slowly on Christmas morning. There was a fresh fallen layer of snow and the day was quiet. It was a Thursday and Kasandra wanted to attend Mass with her parents. I had work waiting for me at my studio, but I had promised to accompany my wife before beginning my tasks. I lay quietly looking at the ceiling, contemplating what I might accomplish in the day. It was still very dark outside, but then it would be dark most of the day. A knock at the door pulled me away from my thoughts.

"You need to get out of bed and help me with the animals." It was Kasandra's father with his morning call to duties.

I rose and got dressed, leaving my very round wife to rest a bit longer. She had but two months to go in our first pregnancy and her energy levels were low much of the time. She could use a few minutes more rest. I kissed her on the forehead and pulled my coat on. Without thinking I put my hand in the pocket and found a piece of paper. I am not in the habit of leaving notes in my coat pocket so I pulled it out to see what it was. The message nearly took my breath away.

"Woodsman, I would appreciate your visiting the Bord family. I have drawn a map to their house on the reverse side of this message. I know you said you were not in a position to provide supplies to families in need, however I noticed that your family has three smoked quarters of venison. Maybe your father-in-law could spare one. I hope to visit with you in six or seven weeks. Merry Christmas, Nicholas."

Turning the message over, I recognized the directions for I had stopped by this house once before. They had an unusual wooden sculpture, more like a polished limb really, and I had wanted to find out where they had acquired it. Nobody was home and I never found my way back to this house.

Kasandra and I received an unexpected surprise following Mass. The priest's closing comment was, "On this blessed day open your hearts to your neighbors as your Father in Heaven opened his to us so many years ago. And finally, a most glorious anniversary to Kasandra and Jameson who were wed in this very church one year ago today. May you all create Christmas memories this day that will last for generations to come." I turned to my wife, who had turned to me and we shared a pleasant kiss which caused the congregation to raise applause.

Christmas and our anniversary were celebrated with an extensive midday meal. Numerous guests, both family and friends, added to our joy and fully consumed one of the venison quarters. When the meal was finished and cleaned, I went to my father-in-law. "Svigerfar, I have been asked to share Christmas by taking a quarter of venison to a family living off the southern road."

"Jameson, in honor of your anniversary I want you to no longer call me Svigerfar. You may call me by my given name, Lars, or address me as 'Far,' as my daughter does. So, who asked you to take our food to another family?"

"Nicholas."

"The same Nicholas who gave you that walking stick?"

"Yes, sir."

My father-in-law thought for a moment, breathing in and out deeply several times before replying, "It is Christmas. Yes, you may have the venison, providing you replace it by next week's end."

I must admit that I am not a great hunter. In fact it is Lars who provides most of the meat for our family, something I will miss when Kasandra and I move to the house at my studio. "Wouldn't it be better if I went hunting with you and did my best to not scare away the deer?"

Lars laughed a deep belly laugh and wrapped his arm around my shoulder, "As long as you do not scare the game away, I will hunt with you."

Since Lars was agreeable, I put on my coat and retrieved one of the two remaining venison quarters. As I passed the door to my room, I stepped in to grab the *Woodsman's* walking stick.

"Going to be *The Woodsman?*" Kasandra asked with a smile.

I smiled in reply and kissed her. She pushed me away, rather she pushed the venison away. I laughed as I picked up the staff and left on my first journey. It was no longer snowing and my heart was light. I remember how good it felt to be going to see someone with a gift they might appreciate.

Approaching the cabin I saw a fine line of smoke coming from the chimney, much thinner than I expected. Looking around the cabin I did not see a wood pile. "Maybe it is in the back," I thought. I knocked on the door. There was no answer, so I knocked again.

"No one is at home," came a small voice from the other side. "We have all flown away."

"I guess I will have to enjoy this side of smoked venison by myself," I called back to the door.

The door opened immediately and I was faced by three young children between the ages of four and eight. "Is that really venison? And may we have some?" the eldest, a girl, asked.

"It is all for you and I would be pleased to cut some for you if I may come inside." I smiled at the three faces. All three children stepped aside to allow my entry, still I could not move.

The rafters of this small cottage were filled with the most extraordinary wood art I had ever seen. My eyes raced around the rest of the cottage. Dozens of pieces of wood in various stages of completion cluttered the small home. In a small alcove to the back of the cottage, a man of about thirty years wrestled with a limb of some kind. He and the wood were soaked in water and he wrestled vigorously, oblivious to my arrival. One of the children grabbed my coat and pulled me inside.

"You promised to cut us some venison," the child said as he tugged on my coat.

"Do you have a knife I can use to cut it?" I asked looking around the kitchen area.

The eldest daughter found a knife and handed it to me. The youngest of the three was a girl and the middle child was a boy. As I cut the meat I introduced myself, "I am the Woodsman of Saint Nicholas. He told me you would enjoy this meat, however he did not tell me your names."

"I am Gerda," the eldest took the honors of introducing everyone. "And this is Fred and the youngest is Anna."

Suddenly their father looked up and was startled to see me in his home. "Who are you and why are you here? Gerda, where is your mother?"

"She went to Missus Youker's to help with the new baby."

"Please excuse my intruding on your work, sir. My name is Jameson Thorpe and I was just bringing some Christmas for the children to enjoy." I stepped toward the man with my hand outstretched.

"One moment, sir, and I will greet you," the young man grunted and twisted the limb in his hands. With a show of incredible strength he reshaped the soaked wood into the design he had chosen and put it down. Wiping his hands on a wet apron, he stood and greeted me. "Roy Brok, sir. Thank you for the venison. It is venison? I did hear that correctly?"

"Yes, it is," I chuckled and shook Roy's hand.

"And you say you work with Saint Nicholas?"

"Yes, he asked me to call on you, but to be honest I would like to speak with you about your work. Why do you create so many objects of art? Do you have an agent who sells them for you?"

"Each piece takes many steps to make it an object of art, as you say. I sell them at street markets and festivals. Enough to keep us fed and healthy. But, no, I have never been approached by what you said, an agent. I have plenty of pieces, do you know of an agent who can find buyers for my work?"

My heart was pounding with excitement and I had to remember that it was Nicholas who sent me here on this day. Looking around I could see no wood for the fire and the meager flame was near death. "It is a bit chilly, don't you think? Where might I find some wood for the fire?"

"Fred, you and Gerda bring in some wood," the father directed his children. "I must apologize. I get lost to the world when I find a limb such as this one. It will be beautiful one day."

"Father," Gerda interrupted, "there is no more wood."

"Roy, if you have an axe and some dry clothes I will help you get some wood. Then tomorrow I can bring you some coal."

"I would appreciate your help with the axe, but I cannot accept your charity."

"It would not be charity, trust me. It would be an investment . . . an investment in your art, for I am an agent." I smiled at Roy's puzzled face.

Roy and I spent the next hour and a half cutting several small trees. He kept inspecting the branches for use in his art and I kept turning him back to cutting. After we had cut enough wood to heat their cottage for several days we returned and found Missus Brok, Rebecca, had returned. After promising to visit again, soon, I left with a skip in my step. Then I had to turn back for I had forgotten *The Woodsman's Staff*.

Over the next ten days, Roy and I examined his work that was ready to sell. We selected six pieces to take to distributors I normally use to sell local work worldwide. I carefully wrapped the pieces and stored them until I could travel to Oslo and Trondheim. During the remaining winter months I visited the Borg family as often as I could. Frequently, I found the wood pile low and Roy engrossed in his art. I actually put a piece of wood he had selected to work on into the fire before he picked up his axe and went out to cut firewood. It might have been a beautiful piece.

February 19, 1891 changed my life as my wife presented me with a healthy baby girl, whom we named Kristine. She was born with fire red hair and a demanding personality. Nicholas arrived the following day, claiming he had not been far away and wanted to visit. Lars and Kasandra greeted Nicholas with near disbelief for they recognized his image but could not believe he was actually visiting. Hannah, my mother-in-law, looked at Nicholas coldly and asked, "Will you be staying for lunch?"

"Hannah," Nicholas replied with a chuckle, "even as a young girl you came straight to the point of the conversation. It must be that you were the eldest of four sisters."

Lars, Kasandra, and I stared at Nicholas in amazement. Even I did not know that Hannah had been this way as a girl. I thought it came from living with Lars for so many years.

"Will you be staying for lunch?" Hannah repeated.

"Thank you, but no, I have another stop to make." He

graciously nodded to Hannah and then turned to me. "Woodsman, may I be of assistance to you with our friend?"

"Only if you can help me get his work to my distributors," I replied.

"When can you leave?" Nicholas responded, his expression quite serious.

"After lunch?"

Nicholas turned back to my mother-in-law, "Hannah, there has been a change in my itinerary. If your invitation is still open, I would love to dine with you."

Kasandra put Kristine in my arms so she could help her mother prepare lunch. Immediately, the child began to scream. I rocked her in my arms, changed her position, and even tried to sing to her. Nothing quieted her. Nicholas lifted her from my arms and she became quiet as soon as he touched her. Holding her in the same manner as I had, he looked down at her and spoke softly. She seemed to be participating in his conversation. Soon she fell asleep and Nicholas, the dear old grandfather, put her in the cradle.

After lunch Nicholas and I walked to my shop where Roy's art was stored. I was astonished to find a beautifully carved sleigh with two reindeer waiting near the door. Entering, Nicholas looked around and smiled. "You could live here quite comfortably."

"I plan to, as soon as I can get Kasandra and Kristine to make the change. I have been working on the living section for months and finished it only last week. It is weather tight, the wood pile is stocked, but the larder is empty."

Nicholas laughed as he helped me load six pieces of art into his sleigh. After securing the door I stepped into the sleigh and noticed how low it was to the ground. "You have very little clearance on this sleigh. How do you get anywhere?"

With a twinkle in his eye Nicholas shook the reins and gave a short whistle. Seconds later I was looking down at Namskogan as it disappeared beneath the clouds. "Where are we going?" Nicholas asked.

"The first stop would be in Trondheim, then two dealers in Oslo." I gasped as I spoke, doing my best to breathe normally.

My knuckles ached with the strain of holding tightly to the airborne sleigh.

I would normally spend several days on the journey to Trondheim, however today, we arrived in less than one hour. The reindeer trotted down the streets with the sleigh gliding along, barely brushing the top of the snow and ice. My distributor, Gunther, was pleased to see me and looked for my usual abundance of Norwegian art but was not so pleased when he saw what I had brought to him.

"It is interesting, I grant you, but I know of no one who might pay anything significant for it," he grumbled. "I am sorry you made the journey, but I do not think I am interested."

"The artist is very talented but not a good business man. He needs the money. You could help him if you took just this one piece for one hundred fifty krone." I watched as the distributor stared at the piece, obviously pondering who he could sell it to at twice the price.

"One hundred," he finally replied.

"I cannot do that. I would have to increase the price on the others just to cover my costs. He is hungry with a young family and he is dedicated. You will be surprised how your customers react to his creations. One-fifty." After my pitch I waited for him to respond. When he did not, I began to re-wrap the piece and leave.

"Okay, one-forty. But only if you bring me more of the tall trolls." He shook his head as he put his hand out. I shook it firmly and smiled. Moments later he returned with an envelope which I put in my pocket without opening it.

I returned a second piece back into the sleigh and we departed toward Oslo. "You did not count the money," Nicholas commented.

"I would never insult a partner by counting the money in front of him," I replied. Nicholas smiled.

It was getting late when we arrived at the first distributor's shop in Oslo. He truly was not interested in the art and indicated that he might not be wanting more trolls, still I could stop by the next time I was in town. The second dealer was closed with a sign on the door that there was an illness in the family. My sigh must have alarmed Nicholas for he asked, "Is it that bad?"

"I sell most of my work with these three dealers. I had hoped for more with Roy's art, it is extraordinary and different. I know the first dealer will want more later, but that will not feed Roy's family now."

"Have you ever been to Bryggen?" Nicholas asked, with a twinkle in his eye. I was learning that his twinkle was a good thing to see.

"It is late, but what do we have to lose? Where is Bryggen?"

As the sleigh sailed westward, toward the last rays of the setting sun, Nicholas explained to me that Bryggen was the shipping district of Bergen, on the west coast. Surrounded by darkness, Nicholas landed his sleigh next to a small shop at the edge of the business district. A light flickered inside. "Select two pieces," he told me as he sprang toward the door of the shop.

"KARL!" Nicholas called out as he opened the door.

A short, stout man with a full beard resting on his vest greeted Nicholas with a tremendous hug. "What brings you here this time of year?" the man asked warmly. Then he saw me and extended his hand, "I am Karl Nielsen. You are welcome to my shop if you can tell me how this scoundrel talked you into riding in his sleigh."

Realizing these two men were very good friends I told the truth, "He did not tell me how we would be traveling. I stepped in and had no choice after that."

Karl laughed with his entire body. When he could speak again, he asked, "Nicholas, what can I do for you this fine evening?"

"Jameson is working with a young artist and I would like you to look at his work. Tell me what you think it is worth."

I unwrapped the pieces I had brought in. Karl looked at them intently. Carefully he lifted each piece and examined it from every angle. Then rubbing his chin he announced, "In New York I could sell these pieces for One hundred twenty, maybe one hundred fifty dollars. In Paris, maybe thee hundred thousand francs. In London, they would use them for match sticks."

"We have three additional pieces with us. What can you do for our young artist?" Nicholas asked with a touch of pleading in his eye.

Karl sighed and walked over to his desk where he bent over some papers and scratched some figures. "I will give you seven hundred forty krones for the lot, PROVIDING you write the artist's history right now and promise to bring me more pieces when I send for them."

I nearly passed out. Never had I received this kind of offer for an unknown artist. Even my well known and accepted artisans did not command this respect from a new dealer. With Karl's permission I sat at his desk and wrote out everything I knew about Roy Brok. Karl read over my shoulder as I wrote and smiled. Nicholas brought the remaining pieces in from the sleigh and beamed as though he were delivering Christmas presents to a deserving child. Business completed, Karl invited Nicholas and me to supper, which was delicious.

It was late that night, or early the next morning, when I crawled under the covers and snuggled close to Kasandra. "Your knees are cold! What are you doing back so soon?" she murmured softly.

"Later. I need to sleep," I whispered and kissed her tenderly. It had been a remarkable day.

My distributor in Oslo, who had not wanted to look at Roy's art, is no longer one of my distributors. Art is a risky business at times and one bad investment can ruin a small distributor. I had not realized as I dealt with this man for years, that his shop was not his own for he owed a considerable amount of money to many investors. It was a small comfort to learn that his lack of interest in Roy's art was not lack of desire but of resources. My second Oslo distributor, Jakob, had suffered the loss of his mother who died suddenly the day before we arrived at his door. He later purchased three of Roy's pieces and continued to support the work of my other clients.

Karl became Roy's largest promoter and also promoted all of the work I could acquire outside of the realm of Norwegian Trolls. "Trolls are very popular," he told me, "but everyone is selling them. I am more interested in art for a discerning eye. Bring me work that shows the heart of the artist."

Many times while Voltik and I traveled the quiet pathways of northern Norway, I have wondered if Nicholas and Karl were in partnership. Over the years that followed, Nicholas directed me toward eleven artists living in poverty, as was Roy. Nine of the eleven artists were accepted by Karl, almost without hesitation. My other distributors accepted some of the work of these and other artists.

Each new artist enjoyed an elevation of his lifestyle and each welcomed me with a hot meal and a soft bed. I came to know their families on a personal basis and my business pursuits became much more than just acquiring and selling folk art. I came to know my older clients better as well and through this more personal relationship my business prospered, as did theirs.

Kasandra and Kristine moved into the house at my studio with the coming of spring, after Kristine was born. Hannah, Kasandra's mother, visited three to four times each week. Kasandra enjoyed these visits, especially when I was traveling, as they gave her time to better establish our house as a home. Hannah would spend hours holding Kristine and offered advice as to the placement of furniture, as well as what furniture needed to be acquired. Kasandra told me her mother spent considerable time looking at the art in my shop, as though it were a museum.

Both Lars and Hannah had been critical of our marriage because they could not understand how I made enough money to support my family. They were less critical as our finances improved with the growth in my clientele. Lars even journeyed with me to take a collection to my distributors in Trondheim, Oslo, and Bryggen.

Lars and Gunther enjoyed each other's company until Gunther and I tried to negotiate a price on the work he wanted. Gunther never agreed to my first request so I started high and he always responded too low. We would come to an agreement we could both appreciate. It was a game of sorts. Lars thought the game was an atrocious waste of time and almost hit Gunther when he made his first offer. Our negotiation nearly stopped with Lars' outburst, but I managed to get him outside talking to Voltik and then restarted the game with Gunther. He was not as amiable the second time and I believe it did cost my clients and me a bit of income; a small bit.

Lars kept more to himself at our second stop, possibly because he was still angry with Gunther. He had little to do with Jakob. Karl, on the other hand was warm and friendly to everyone, including my father-in-law. As we left Karl's shop Lars asked, "Why cannot all men be open and honest like this Karl?"

"Many are, Lars," I replied. "Each in their own way being true to their own nature. Each conducts his business according to his own personality and how happy he is with his life."

"You are saying Gunther is not happy and Karl is very happy?"

"Karl is very content with his life, yes. Gunther . . . well, Gunther grew up bartering for anything he needed to acquire or wished for. When you are on the losing side of too many negotiations, you become over protective of what you have. Besides, when he purchases a work of art he is taking the risk that he can sell it. If he does, then good. If he does not, he has an expensive piece of firewood. I have spent years getting to know my distributors and while each is very different, I trust them and appreciate what they can do for my clients and my family."

"You have a strange way of earning your money," Lars humphed and sat back to enjoy the ride home.

"Happy Anniversary, Woodsman."

I recognized the voice but was not in the state of mind to appreciate the sentiment. "Good morning, Nicholas. What do you mean 'Happy Anniversary'?" I asked as I turned around from my work bench.

"It was one year ago you agreed to carry that staff, the 'Woodsman's Staff,' " he replied with a twinkle in his eye.

I thought for a moment and smiled just a bit. It was December 7, one year and one day after I met this old storyteller. It had been a profitable year and a year filled with adventures I could have never imagined I would be a part of.

"If you have the time, I would like you to meet a friend of mine," the old man beamed. I could tell this was another of his adventures.

"Let me tell Kasandra I am leaving," I acknowledged somewhat reluctantly. "When should I tell her we will return?"

"Oh, these visits are usually brief. You should be back by supper," he replied, then hesitated. "But to be honest, they often last several days. Would you mind asking your wife for some of her delicious oatmeal cookies?"

Kasandra's face reflected something between resignation and a hopeless sense of loss. These journeys with Nicholas weighed heavily on her state of mind. She never knew where I was, when I would return, or even if I was okay or lying injured in the woods somewhere. She knew Nicholas would never put any person in a harmful situation, still there were times when he had been a bit flighty in his actions.

"Let us go," I said, as I handed Nicholas a sack which he immediately put his hand in to. "She is not happy, but she is understanding."

Nicholas pulled a bar of oatcake from the bag and turned over in his hand. He nibbled the corner and his face lit up like a Christmas night. "DELICIOUS! What is this marvelous cake?"

"It is an oatmeal cookie mixed with Kasandra's special

spices and baked as a block or a cake. I am glad you like it," I replied with growing impatience. "Are we going?"

"Yes, yes," he almost stumbled as we left my shop. "Orlf will love these!"

I hesitated in my step, and would have liked to turn around right then, but I had learned to trust Nicholas and finished tying my coat as I stepped into his sleigh. "So, where are we going today?"

"We are walking, come along." His eyes were twinkling like a cold night sky ablaze with stars.

He dropped the cake back into the sack with a smile as we walked north through the village and beyond. After an hour, or so, we turned onto an almost indiscernible trail to the west, through the forest. Snow on the ground was undisturbed by animal or man. The only sign that this was a way into the woods was the spacing of trees which formed a natural corridor. Eventually we came upon a ring of five rocks, each shaped roughly like a ball about one meter across. Nicholas sat on one of the rocks and pointed to the one to his right, indicating that I should sit as well. It was now early afternoon and my stomach was wondering why I had not packed something to eat. My eyes floated toward the sack Nicholas was holding on his lap when a large figure appeared opposite us, outside the circle of rocks. Nicholas waved his hand telling me to stay seated. His smile helped me relax.

Standing in front of us was a troll. A Norwegian troll standing nearly three meters tall. Most of the creature's height was torso, very round but also very firm in appearance, except his apparently well fed stomach which looked like an extremely large cabbage. His legs were slightly more than one meter in length and looked like tree trunks with knees. Enormous feet resembling river barges with bulbous toes were covered by mats of hair. The creature's arms were exceptionally long and thin, compared to the rest of his body, and carried massive hands which hung relaxed just above his knees. His head also resembled a large cabbage, though not quite as large as his stomach, and had exaggerated features. His nose was long and egg-shaped, his ears large and appeared as sails on either side of his head. But his eyes were more remarkable than the rest of his presence, for they were soft brown in colour and whispered a kindness such as I have never seen. The troll's hair was scraggly, to say the best, and varied in length from his shoulders to halfway down his back. He was cloaked in a deer skin tunic extending almost to his knees.

"Orlf, this is my very good friend Jameson," Nicholas proceeded with introductions without standing. "Jameson, I am pleased to introduce you to Orlf, current king of the Northern Norwegian Troll Kingdom."

Orlf nodded politely and then planted his body on the rock opposite Nicholas and me.

"You said 'Northern Norwegian Troll Kingdom'?" I asked, not believing what was happening.

"Oh, they have a much more involved name for their kingdom, but I have trouble pronouncing it and you would not understand it either," Nicholas admitted. He then reached into the sack and removed a piece of cake, offering it to Orlf. Nicholas extended his arm full length and leaned into the circle just a bit. Orlf reached over with one of his long arms and accepted the gift without expression of any kind. I watched as Orlf's eyes shifted to me and then back to Nicholas before he raised the cake to his nose. A gentle sniff, which sounded like a horse's snort, and the giant troll smiled. He then cautiously placed the cake on his tongue and his entire face lit up with delight. "Very good. More!"

"I must apologize that I did sample one of the cakes, but this sack is for you," Nicholas confessed, leaning into the circle but not rising.

What followed was about an hour of pleasantries during which I learned that Orlf's wife had just had a baby. Lundar is their ninth child and seventh son. I could see the pride in Orlf's face as he talked about all of his children, his wife, his father, grandfather, and uncle. The last three were no longer alive, but their spirits continued to guide Orlf through his daily duties as leader of the troll kingdom. Orlf then sat quietly and stared at me, whereupon Nicholas whispered, "He is waiting to hear about your family."

My discussion lasted only about ten minutes. I explained, "My family is still very young. My wife, Kasandra, and I have been wed for only two years and we have but one daughter. I hope to have more children, especially a son, with God's blessing."

Orlf considered my report and looked to Nicholas. "Natasha is well and sends her love to you and your family. All of your friends in Alapuolella Pohjantähti send you their love as well and want to know when you will bring your family for another visit?"

Orlf thought before replying, "In warm time when Lundar can run down your pathways."

"We shall expect you and hold a great celebration when you arrive," Nicholas smiled.

Orlf shook the sack. It was empty, as it had been for the last six times he had looked for another treat. "These good," he repeated. He looked at me and then at Nicholas. "Deer gone."

"Have you moved your village?" Nicholas asked.

"No." Orlf retreated into his memories for several minutes. "Ungar, third son born in village."

"Have your hunters gone on a long hunt?" Nicholas questioned.

Orlf thought for a moment then replied, "Not this cold. Went for two moons when warm came last."

"I suggest you watch for signs of a herd on your return home," Nicholas advised Orlf. "The deer will not be moving this time of year and you must have food for the cold. Find a herd and lead them to your village. You should get some help from your family to do this."

"Orlf carry one, two if small," the King replied with a grin.

"Yes, but you might scare the herd away. Wait until you have help and lead the herd home," Nicholas encouraged. "It is growing dark."

Orlf looked at the sky and then cast his eyes around the forest. Sighting an unusual tree, very lean with smooth bark, the troll rose and lumbered over to it. Looking down at his hands, he selected a finger with a long nail and ran his finger nail around a small branch. The branch fell into his hand and he returned with his harvest. Using the same finger, he cut a section from the branch about four inches long, laying the rest of the branch on the ground beside him. He then examined his hands again and selecting a different finger, used his finger nail to scrape one of the ends of the wood he was holding. With careful precision he scraped the wood fibers loose and then twirled them together. Taking a deep breath and letting it go with a sigh, he looked to Nicholas and then to me. Nicholas shook his head and my face was clouded with confusion. The big man then rubbed his first finger and thumb on his stone seat for several seconds. He quickly grabbed the twisted fibers and blew on them gently. The wood burst into flame and gave a tremendous light.

"Thank you," Nicholas acknowledged with a smile. "What else do we need to discuss?"

I sat completely dumbfounded, staring at the burning wood, which Orlf had positioned on the vacant stone between him and Nicholas. Their conversation lasted for hours. After about thirty minutes, I interrupted and asked Orlf if I could see the branch he had placed on the ground. He cut his eyes at me, not sure whether or not to share.

"His wife, Kasandra, made the cakes," Nicholas commented.

Orlf then smiled brightly and handed the branch to me. While the other two talked I examined the branch. The cut section, which was as clean a cut as I have ever seen, was as wide as my two fingers and had a slightly damp feel to it. I withdrew a small knife from my pouch and tried scraping the fibers as Orlf had done with his finger nail. When he saw what I was doing he burst out laughing, a roaring deep bass laugh that filled the forest. Resuming his conversation with Nicholas, he took the branch from me. Quickly, and expertly, he cut three more sections from the branch and scraped one end of each of the sections. After twirling the fibers together on the third piece, Orlf presented the collection to me, extending his arm full length so that his palm was open almost in my lap. I accepted his gift with a silent nod and smile.

When Orlf and Nicholas finished their conversation, we all sat in absolute silence for nearly a quarter of an hour. The Troll King then stood, picking up the last of the tree branch. Handing the branch to me he nodded his head slightly and left.

Nicholas stood and patted his stomach contentedly announcing, "What a splendid visit. Do you suppose Kasandra has any supper left?"

"It will be nearly breakfast time before we get home!" I protested.

Nicholas smiled, picked up the burning troll candle and snuffing the flame with his fingers, turned down the path we had used earlier. His small sleigh with two reindeer was waiting just ten meters away.

~~~~~~~~~~~~~~~~~~~~~~~~~~~~

I am not sure when I became accustomed to the unscheduled visits of Nicholas. This man who had changed my life so significantly would appear day and night, without warning. If I was working, he would stand at the door and wait until I saw him, but at night he would simply sit outside the house in his magnificent sleigh. His presence is always felt, even through the deepest sleep or my most intriguing dreams - some of which I believe are inspired by this unusual friend.

Visits are rarely a matter of wanting to just visit. He almost always has an agenda, something I need to do for him. Sometimes he wants me to visit a family that has either made an unusual piece of art or might have found a unique piece among family heirlooms. These families are always in need and selling a single piece brings much needed income. I also have learned to work with local churches to help families correct long term problems. I rarely find a family looking for a handout, rather they are looking for a hand up. Once on their feet, they repay the kindness shown to them by helping others.

"You need to be careful how you share your gifts, Woodsman," Nicholas told me one day on the ride home from one of his expeditions where a man was cold in his response to our efforts to work with him. "Many people will take advantage of your generous nature. It will be okay, for a while, as you shrug off their ingratitude, but it can gnaw away at you after a time. I have also seen your eyes when you find someone who truly needs and wants your help. You sparkle like sunlight on a field of ice as you work with them and develop a plan for their work and future. There are also those whom you may not be aware of; those who do not react to your generosity and help, but ponder it. Then, when they are ready, they take the assistance you have given them and begin a new life - built on your gifts to them. Surely you can see when someone responds favorably to you. But you can never know when someone simply does not care for their life and what you have done for them, or if they are pondering the value of your gift in their life. Always share your talents openly and without prejudice. Above all, my friend, never expect anything in return for your efforts."

I considered his words carefully, pondering on this advice and letting it sink into my thoughts. I do expect to be paid for my trade in local art, it is how I earn a living, but there is something of merit in what Nicholas told me. While I can make a living I can also change lives, most often for the better, but I need to offer my help without thinking about any return. This is very difficult when I need new tools or Kasandra needs something, but even these needs seem to resolve themselves.

Orlf's candle humiliated me. Using the three pieces he cut for me I tried diligently, and unsuccessfully to scrape wood fibers into a wick. The one we used during our meeting lasted for months and never dimmed or seemed to exhaust its fuel. Knowing I would need additional resources to continue to study this Troll Candle, I went in search of trees. I located some trees like Orlf used to make his candle about ten kilometers from my home. My first study with the new branches was to split a section down the middle. I discovered a very light sap that would glow with a gentle flame when lit.

The light given off by this flame was unusually bright yet there was very little heat. While I was investigating this phenomenon, I left the split stick burning on my workbench where my daughter, Kristine, discovered it. She was infatuated with the dancing of the flame and grabbed the burning stick before I could get back to her. The half of the stick that was in her hand stopped burning yet the exposed half continued to flicker, without burning her! It did, however, singe her hair slightly when she turned her head. Kasandra scolded me severely for allowing Kristine opportunity to touch it.

Unable to scrape the fibers into a wick, I resolved to insert a more traditional wick into the wood. Using wood I had harvested locally, I cut several pieces as long as my hand is wide and bore a hole through the core. I then stuffed a piece of cotton rope through the hole, much like threading a needle with a ship line. Eventually I accomplished my plan, actually creating two wooden candles with cotton wicks. After admiring my work, I held one of the candles with only a few centimeters of rope exposed to the fire in our cottage. The rope burned and smoked furiously for a few minutes and went out. The exposed rope was completely spent by the flame. Frustrated I left both the burnt candle and the second candle on my workbench.

About a week later I moved the two pieces of wood so I could work and noticed the wick in the unspent candle had changed colour. The white rope was now golden. Rubbing my finger across the wick I felt dampness, yet the oil did not leave any residue on my fingers. Exploding with curiosity, I put the wick to the fire and it glowed with a gentle flame which was incredibly bright. Filled with hope I squashed the flame with my fingers and found it to be considerably cooler than a traditional candle, even cool enough to not burn small hands.

Nicholas had told me about the tokens left by his other *Woodsmen*; Andrew's stick and Abram's coin. Knowing the wood for these remarkable troll candles was uncommon and difficult to identify in the forest, I decided this unique object would be my token for those I have the opportunity to help. A glowing memory to help people find the light in a new tomorrow.

Traveling with Nicholas gave me a fresh view of the men, women, and families around Norge (Norway). I saw them not as simply artisans or customers but as people struggling to make a living just as I was. The young children were cute, even with their wet noses in need of constant attention, and the men and women were parents - just like me! This realization made my journeys more comfortable, for I was now traveling to visit with friends. Yes, we did business together, however I came to know the children and enjoyed watching them grow.

My own family grew as Kasandra and I magically managed to have two more children. I say 'magically' for my bride says I am never home enough to have children. A second daughter, Inga, came to us when Kristine was only twenty-one months old. Kasandra lost two babes in the womb and we thought two daughters were to be our blessing. But when Inga was about to turn five years old, Artur was born. A son.

Somehow news of my children spread through my community of customers and artists. Many members of my professional family chastised me for leaving my wife alone with a young infant. "My wife's mother is at our home with her and would rather I earn a living than sit and wash little behinds," I explained. Business continued to be strong as men wished they could travel with me and women sent their blessings to the mother of my children.

Christmas became a very special holiday in our house. As the children grew up, we would decorate a big tree with Troll Candles. Kristine found that soaking the wick in dyes (usually green or blue) before putting it in the stick caused the candle to glow with the colour of the dye. This made our trees even more festive. On Christmas Eve we would fix a big vat of rice porridge to go with our mutton ribs and cabbage. Bowls of carrots, cauliflower, and sprouts helped to fill Lars', my father-in-law's, appetite. Before going to bed the children would take bowls of the rice porridge to the barn where Fjøsnissen (Nisse), our little Christmas gnome, cared for the animals. We never lost an animal in the Winter so I suppose Nisse was happy. Nicholas would stop and bring presents for each of us, even Lars. I enjoyed watching Nicholas shimmer as he arranged gifts and nibbled on the sand kager cookies the children left for him. I made sure there were carrots and treats for the reindeer.

Christmas Morning found our family in church where Kasandra and I renewed our vows, every year. Our small community looked forward to this small act and when we thought we would not do it one year, the minister convinced us otherwise.

Artur was barely six months old when I found a note on my workbench, "*You should visit Gunther Roland. He lives a community called Harstad, outside of Trondenes. I know this is a ways to travel, but you will enjoy the visit. Nicholas.*" I had never heard of this community, fortunately I was able to locate Harstad on a map. Karl Nielsen, my distributor in Bryggen, had suggested I visit a friend of his in Ankenes, which my eyes told me as I surveyed the map, was not too distant from Harstad. The thought crossed my mind that Nicholas and Karl were working in unison to get me to visit this man Gunther Roland.

Curiosity about Gunther began to fill my thoughts as I planned my journey to visit artists and customers in spring 1901. I resolved to extend my travel to Ankenes and then onward to Trondenes. The first part of my journey was without surprise. My visits were all greeted with warmth and friendship and my cart filled quickly with new treasures, even as it emptied of those I delivered. When I arrived at the shop of Adam Smythe, in Ankenes, I had a vast assortment of art for him to examine.

Adam Smythe, the English friend of Karl, told me, "I was walking to the shop where I was employed, just down the road from my home in Berkshire, when I turned toward to the coast, quite by mistake. Two years later I woke up in Ankenes and was the owner of this shop. At that time I sold delicates to ladies of means and was most unhappy. I met Karl on one of his outings and he introduced me to this world of trading art. That was twenty-three years ago and I have never been happier, except when, at the age of twelve, I stole a kiss from a gorgeous young lady." His eyes twinkled and as a very attractive lady entered he quickly added, "But please don't tell my wife." Wrapping his arms around the lady, he stole a kiss and beamed with delight.

We spent the afternoon examining every piece of art I had in my cart and he purchased six pieces from four different artists. While we settled accounts, I looked around his shop and discovered a ship that was both unusual and beautiful. It was a Viking war ship, carved in incredible detail. It took very little imagination to place yourself in one of its seats and pull on a massive oar.

"I am told, and it can be verified by examination, that the entire work is carved from a single piece of wood. The oars, even the sail were released as a single carving," Adam remarked as he handed me an envelope. "I do not know who the artist is but he is a remarkable man of patience and insight."

I examined the work more closely and was able to match the grain of the wood through the ship into the oars and realized, upon inspection, that the sail was not added but was part of the carving. Even the tiller worked. "A remarkable piece of art," I sighed.

Adam and his wife were kind enough to put me up for the night and I left early the next morning for Trondenes. While the distance between Ankenes and Trondenes was short on the map, it took a full day to work around the lakes, fiords, and bridges. Voltik, my cart pony, had taken to complaining about each new bridge; he was not fond of all the water. I took lodging in Harstad and went in search of Mister Gunther Roland the next morning.

My search ended quickly as my innkeeper knew of Trondenes and upon arriving in this delightful community I learned that everyone knew everyone else. I was directed to a small house near the end of a pier which looked out over the water. Reaching for the door, I was stunned when it opened abruptly and a beautiful young woman appeared in its place. Her long light brown hair framed brown eyes which sparkled in the morning sunlight and a smallish nose made even less by a beaming smile. She stood barely above my shoulders and presented a remarkable vision accented by a bright blue dress and pristine white apron.

Almost giggling, she called back into the house, "Father, there is a gentleman to see you." She then skipped down the lane, my eyes following every movement, every swish of her hair.

"May I help you?"

A stern man's voice pulled me out of my daze. Turning my head, I found a man of average height, broad shoulders, bearded chin, balding head, and the same sparkling eyes as the young lady who had just left. "Ex . . . Excuse me, sir," I stammered. "I am looking for Mister Gunther Roland."

"I am he," the man replied.

"My name is Jameson Thorpe, sir, and I have been asked to visit you."

"Come in and visit, Mister Jameson Thorpe. May I ask who sent you and for what reason?"

"I believe the man would prefer to remain anonymous . . ." I said as I entered the humble cottage. My eyes immediately fell on two objects at the same time. On the mantle over the fire was a belt of sleigh bells and on the table to the left of the fireplace was a partially carved ship, or rather, a large block of wood with an English sailing ship emerging from it. Adapting my response to these discoveries I continued, "My friend's name is Nicholas and I must assume he asked me to visit with you because you are an incredible artist and I buy and sell art."

"Nicholas? He is supposed to find a young man strong enough to marry my daughter, Florence. But he sends me an art collector?"

"You say you need a man 'strong enough'?"

"You saw her; every man in three counties wants to court her, yet none can last more than an hour. Her mother died when she was born. Being a sailor I was off at sea, so they placed my daughter in an orphanage. I came home from the sea to raise her. She never had the training of a woman but plenty influence from old sailors like me. Never has there been a girl as confident and demanding of confidence in a man. And if they get past her, they must deal with me! I want to play with my grandchildren so they must live close to me!"

"I can offer no suggestions for your daughter, but I have many questions about your ships." Looking around the room I saw many ships of different designs. Each ship meticulously carved and finished with realistic details. I quickly counted fourteen ships in the main room of the small cottage.

"My ships." Gunther waited for me to complete my survey and turn my attention back to him. "Your first question is how and then why? The 'why' is why not? I have nothing else to do except tend my small garden and animals and I enjoy the carving. How? When I was younger, before Florence was born, I sailed around the world in a merchant ship. I was first mate. When we stopped at ports, I would take time to visit with the people. I found men in the Orient who carved images inside of images. They used ivory and whale bone. Each time I visited with them they would show me more of how they did their work and their tools."

Gunther stood and unrolled a cloth filled with small carving knives. Some were mere picks yet others were curved blades sharp enough to slice the hardest wood in any fashion an artist might direct with their hands. He had seventeen different tools to do the detail on his miniature ships.

"As a man of the sea," Gunther continued, "I love ships. I began carving my ships when I took Florence from the orphanage and brought her to this cottage. I have no family to help raise my daughter and I will not ask the church to do it for me, so I have time. Now, what can you, Mister Art Collector, do for me?"

"I do not collect art. I purchase and sell art through several dealers. One dealer, not far from here, has one of your ships and would very much like to meet you."

"That is nice. Why would I want to sell my ships with you?"

"You obviously are not in need of money or you would have sold them long ago," I began as I shifted from visit to business. "Your art inspires greatness in others. When I look at your ships, I am in awe and with little effort I can feel the pull on the oars and the wind below the sails. Your ships represent the freedom and challenge of the ocean and inspire dreams. I would not begin to try to sell your ships for the wealth they could bring you but for the wonder they would bring to people who see them and who might be fortunate enough to own one."

"And how would you do this, friend of Nicholas?"

"With your help, I would select just three ships and take them to my dealer in Bryggen. I would have him appraise them and purchase them from me for a fair price. I would then bring you half of what he pays me."

Gunther thought for a moment and then shrugged his shoulders, "Why not? They only collect dust in my cottage."

We then looked around the cottage and Gunther told me stories about many of the ships he had carved. Some were from his imagination, others were replicas of ships he had sailed on. He explained that the simpler ships took about four weeks to carve while the more detailed ships were done over a year. His aging hands could now work the intricate detail only in small amounts of time before needing to rest. In addition to the fourteen I saw in the big room, he brought twenty more down from his loft.

We had just finished wrapping the fourth ship and put it in my cart when Florence returned. She looked through the works in my cart casually, not paying any attention to her father or me. I found I was unable to breathe when she was around; she carried such a sensual aire about her.

"Mister Thorpe . . . MISTER THORPE!"

I shook off Florence's enchantment as her father was yelling at me. "Yes?"

"When will you return?"

"I make this journey twice each year, so I will return in the fall . . . unless I need to speak with you sooner."

"No, the fall will be acceptable, unless you find a husband for my daughter - then yesterday will not be soon enough."

I laughed and shook Gunther's hand vigorously. "May I tell my friend in Ankenes that I found his ship maker?"

"Does he have a son?"

"Not that I know of."

"You can tell him anyway," Gunther laughed and waved as he and Florence returned to their cottage.

I offered Gunther Roland's ships to Adam Smythe and Karl Nielsen. Adam was excited to learn I had found the man who made these miraculous ships but did not feel his clientele would be willing to pay what they were worth. Karl, however, mesmerized by the craftsmanship and art in the ships immediately purchased all four I had with me. "My markets in London and New York will pay handsomely for these. You bring me whatever the artist wishes to sell and I will pay whatever he demands, within reason of course."

My association with Nicholas had brought me another artist and additional income. Since becoming *The Woodsman* for Nicholas my business had almost doubled, but so had my travel. I had two new distributors and eight new artists who constantly created new works. In order to keep up with everyone, I had to travel my semiannual route three times a year. Voltik, my cart pony, complained about the trips and expressed concern about getting a larger cart. I believe we would have required a second pony if my business had grown any larger.

My wife's father, Lars, thought all the growth was fantastic. "I still do not understand all that you do, but you obviously do it very well. Maybe you should consider hiring an assistant!"

I pondered this comment for several weeks and many short trips. An assistant would give me more time for my growing children, yet I might lose contact with those who were making me successful. My decision was made for me when a local buyer asked how my son was doing. Artur was very young at the time and had suffered a bump on the head when he fell from a wood pile. My buyer remembered and asked about my son with genuine concern. Artur was not hurt badly, but my heart sang with relief as the thoughts of hiring an assistant floated away. I realized at that moment that my success was due to my relationship with my artists and buyers. I would have to carefully consider taking on any more buyers, distributors, or artists for success has its costs.

While my business was increasing and becoming more demanding of my time, I set in place certain rules or procedures. One of these unwritten guides was to take a week for my family when I returned from visiting the distributors in the South. The trip often took ten to fourteen days, depending upon the load and the weather, and I needed the rest as well as time with Kasandra and the children.

I had just returned from a visit to my distributors. The late November weather had been mild but changed to bitter cold as December arrived, making my return slow and exhausting. My heart sank into my toes my first morning home, when Artur found a card with the all too familiar writing on it. I was sitting at the table talking with Kristine and Inga. Kasandra had to interpret part of their rolling conversation so I did not get too lost, when three-year-old Artur interrupted and brought the card to me. I plummeted into a well, not hearing anything around me, as I took the card from my son. I could not bring myself to turn it over and read the message. I needed time with MY family! Kasandra must have seen the look of despair on my face, for the next thing I was aware of was her standing in front of me reading the message.

"This one can wait a couple days, maybe take the children with you," she smiled as she handed me the card.

I took the card and began reading with a heavy sigh, "Woodsman . . ." there were days I despised this label, "after you have rested, there is a family, Jorgen, in the Heggli community who might benefit from a visit. Take your family, it would be a delightful outing." 'Take your family,' this was new, I had never taken the family on one of these missions. Looking up I saw Kasandra's eyes smiling down at me. "Why not? The Feast Day of Saint Nicholas is in two days," I agreed.

I did not know what to take for I knew nothing of the Jorgen's circumstances. My wife, who does have a most generous heart, assembled a feast in three baskets wrapped in twice as many blankets. We left about ten o'clock, as the sky lightened. Kristine sang a song that kept rhythm with the clop of Voltik's hooves, whom I know wondered why the family was going out on such a cold day.

By the time we arrived in the Heggli community, we were all singing and laughing with warm hearts and cold noses. I asked a man on the road for the Jorgen family and was directed back the way we had come, about one kilometer. Arriving at a small farm, hidden behind a hill, we were welcomed by four young children. The eldest, a girl about eight years old, greeted us, "Good Saint Nicholas Day, traveler. What can we do for you?"

Without hesitation Kasandra replied, "Good Saint Nicholas Day to you as well. We have three baskets of food and were looking for the family Jorgen who was said to be setting a feast for this wonderful day."

"A feast day it is, Missus, and as this is a day of generous hearts, you are welcome to join us at our table," a young woman offered as she joined the children.

I began lifting the children from the cart when a man suddenly appeared. He stood slightly taller than I, with the broad shoulders of a working man and a smile that began at his chin, wrapped across his face and shone out through his eyes. His forehead was damp with perspiration and he wiped his hand on his trousers before offering it to me. "Tormod Jorgen. Welcome to our humble home and meager feast."

Looking around at the immaculately kept farm and laughing children, I wondered did Nicholas send me here to help this family or did he send this family to help me? I introduced myself and my family as I handed a blanket-wrapped basket to Tormod. He was puzzled by the package but took it inside. Kasandra took another and I brought the third as Issa Jorgen, wife and mother, took Artur by the hand.

The feast was wonderful, barely enough food to feed both families, yet nobody suffered any hunger and a blooming fellowship united both families as one. As the light was quickly fading, I lit three troll candles which filled the cottage with a soft glow. I learned that Tormod had been working on the railway in the south when he suffered a back injury and had to return to his family farm. He could work the farm but had to rest frequently through the day.

"What do you do while you rest?" I asked.

"If the children are around, I tell them stories. When the children are not available, I look at the world God has given me and give Him thanks."

"Children, what do you think of your father's stories?" I asked the gaggle playing around us.

"Father, will you tell us one now?" a daughter pleaded.

Tormod began speaking with his children and before I knew it, both families were sailing on a great three-masted schooner into icy waters searching for a magic serpent. I felt the chill of the wind and icy waters splashing around us. I trembled with fear as a serpent raised high over the small ship and heaved a sigh of relief when I learned that the serpent was friendly.

"Tormod, have you ever considered writing your stories so

others might read and learn from them?" I asked as the children went back to playing.

"Who would want to read my stories?"

"Parents around the world are searching for stories like yours to tell to their children."

"I have no paper and I do not know how I would have them published. We have no money for such things."

"Kristine, would you please look in the box in the front of the cart and bring the pack of paper and some pencils for Mister Jorgen." I smiled with anticipation as Kristine ran out to our cart. "I have a friend in Bryggen who will help us find a publisher for you. It might take some time, but it will not hurt your back and they will be a treasure for your children."

"I will see that he writes the stories," Issa assured me.

Tormod told two more stories before we collected our empty baskets and returned to our cart. Voltik's clopping was the only sound we heard on the journey home. Quiet frequently intensifies the cold, however this day I felt warmer inside than I had in a very long time.

Six months later, I received a package which contained twenty handwritten stories. I took the package to Karl Nielsen who read them with tears streaming down his face amid roars of laughter. "These stories will be published," he assured me.

I could not wait to tell Tormod about Karl's reaction. Kasandra, the children and I went to visit the Jorgen family but found nobody at home. We went into Heggli and found Issa and the girls selling beautiful candles at a local bazaar. The children had been melting bits of old candles together with colored wax they had found at their church. The candles were festive and useful. Suddenly everyone went running to an area near the center of the bazaar. Tormod was telling stories to the entire village. As I listened, I thought of another storyteller I heard years before and how listening to his tales had changed my life.

My two daughters, Kristine and Inga, share incredible imaginations. One of them will begin an adventure telling a story and the other will immediately join the fantasy, escalating the plot. One of their favorite props for stories is The Woodsman's Staff. It has not been my habit to carry it, I rarely used a walking stick, but through their investigation of the top of the staff I learned why I should carry it.

One winter evening, after the sun had completed its brief visit, the girls began complaining about the dark. Their story of the moment needed a light shining down upon them from high overhead. Inga had noticed the hole in the top of the staff and it took no time at all for the two girls to drop a burning troll candle into the staff. These candles burn with a mesmerizing glow to begin with, but when the crystal in the top of the staff caught this unusual light, it filled the room with a magical glow. There was not a single corner of our home that was not illuminated with the softest light I had ever seen. I stared at the crystal in amazement, yet the light never hurt my eyes. Rather, it drew me into a world I could have never imagined without the help of my daughters.

Three weeks after my daughters discovered the light of The Woodsman's Staff, Kasandra asked me to take a basket of cakes to her parents. The sun was still above the horizon and a line of winter clouds was rolling in with the darkness. Artur volunteered to go with me on this errand. Appreciative of his company, I agreed. Without a thought, my six-year-old son pulled on his coat and picked up the staff, along with four troll candles.

"Your grandparents live only three kilometers up the road," I explained, puzzled by his actions.

"Then we should get going," Artur replied.

I relented and allowed him to carry the staff and candles. As we walked, I watched the clouds push the sun aside and snow began to fall with our arrival at the home of Lars and Hannah, Kasandra's parents. It had been my intent to deliver the package and return home. Hannah, however, had been preparing cakes for a church social and our opinions were required. Lars had a multitude of questions about my business and Nicholas. We must have been visiting for almost two hours when a knock came to their door.

"My children are missing!" a woman cried out as Lars opened the door.

Immediately Hannah began warming the woman and Lars pulled his coat on. "Where were they last known to be?" Lars asked, pulling his hat around his ears.

"They were taking the Johannsan boy home but never returned. And now the snow is falling so fast I fear they have lost their way." The woman was in tears.

"Artur, you wait here and help Hannah," I instructed my son.

His reply was to put his coat on and hand me a troll's candle.

"A delightful idea, but what good will a troll candle do in this weather?" I asked, with more than a touch of confusion.

"Put it in the staff," he replied.

Remembering the uncanny glow produced by the crystal and a troll candle, I immediately lit a candle and dropped it into the top of the staff. As we stepped outside the light pulsated with the wind and then seemed to glow more strongly toward one direction. Lars went the opposite direction to get more help and did not see the beam, but Artur did. The two of us followed the light. Several times the candle almost went out but always came back, flickered somewhat, and then pointed our course.

After nearly an hour of pushing through a growing blizzard we happened upon a fallen tree with four children huddled beneath it. "An angel has come to save us," one of the children cried out as we approached.

"I am not an angel, but I am here to take you home," I smiled.

"No, we saw your light coming. We knew you were an angel and we would be okay," the child insisted.

Artur and I took the children back to their mother at Hannah's table, led every step by the light in The Woodsman's Staff. Their mother exploded with tears of relief as we entered the cottage. She had all but given up when Lars returned after only twenty minutes, unable to make any headway through the storm.

"How did you find them in this weather?" Lars and Hannah both asked, filled with amazement.

Artur looked up and smiled, "A bit of the Magic of Christmas, right, Far?" He then reached into the pocket of my coat and pulled out a Troll's Candle. Giving it to the girl who had called us an angel, he told her, "Keep this candle near you. It can light the way for an angel."

"I believe you are right," I agreed. "But your mother will be worried senseless if we do not get home. Lars, Hannah, I believe you can care for your guests without our help." I then grabbed onto Artur's shoulder and we disappeared into the white night. I knew this journey well and did not need the light of the staff, but its soft beam took us to our door and turned into a wonderful heart-warming glow as we stepped into the waiting arms of three anxious ladies.

[5] My route to visit with customers and artists had grown too long to do three times a year, so I made shorter routes and went back to twice each year. I was preparing to journey on my longest route, which included a visit to an artist I met on my last trip, when Nicholas appeared. After some casual pleasantries, always part of Nicholas' visits, he came to the point of this visit.

"What direction do you travel?"

"I will be going west over the mountains then north to a small village beyond Kiruna, the hamlet of Jukkasjärvi. I found a man near there last year who does beautiful work. Why do you ask?"

"That is a very good direction. After you finish with this

---

[5] The story which follows is adapted from "A Task for Saint Nicholas" beginning on page 79 of "Finding Nicholas, secrets of santa revealed by his woodsmen" by E. Gale Buck (c) 2011 by the Silver Wreath Incorporated.

craftsman you speak of, would you mind turning east to a village called Valtoc?"

"I never heard of it. Is there someone there I should meet?"

"Actually, no. I would like to see the village and meet the people. I am thinking that if I were in your company I might learn some secrets of this village."

I stared at Nicholas, pondering what my friend was not telling me. "I can do that. Where do I meet you?"

"I was hoping to travel with you for the entire journey. I do not often get to see the villages this time of year."

"I will ask Kasandra to add some more meat and bread to my basket. Let's go inside and tell her the news." I laughed with puzzlement as we went into the cottage. My wonderful wife added a few biscuits to my basket but her face showed heightened concern when Nicholas and I left. I believe she was worried about what mischief my unexpected companion might bring about.

Nicholas is an extremely warm hearted man and his very presence changes the world around him. During the first two days men, women, and children surrounded him every time we stopped. Even the people I was trying to do business with left our conversation to meet Nicholas or listen to his stories. No matter what he did to stay in the background, people were attracted to him as though by magic. My work came to a standstill!

Suddenly, on the third day, barely anyone gave him a second look. I was able to resume my work with customers and artists and noticed that only occasionally did a child, or more rarely an adult, talk with him. When I visited with a new artist in Jukkasjärvi, Nicholas' childlike charm was a distraction but later served as an asset as the artist's entire family fell in love with him. He even gave the children, twin girls, Troll Candles before we left.

After leaving Jukkasjärvi, we continued to Valtoc where I saw a side to this remarkable man which I had never imagined. Valtoc was once a thriving village, however due to a catastrophe in the family which dominated it, the life of this community had shriveled up.

Nicholas immediately clashed with the leader of the village. I feared Nicholas was about to be pommeled by the larger man. The childlike charm so characteristic of this gentle man I traveled with disappeared. He became a formidable force focusing on a single purpose. For several days we tried to talk with villagers and draw them out. Only one man, who had been a boy when the problem began, recognized Nicholas and gave us aid. With this man's help, Nicholas reawakened the spirit of the village and brought life back into it.

I have often wondered about the miraculous timing of a new minister appearing in that village. As Nicholas, a bishop of the church, conducted services in an old church which was more shell than building, a young minister arrived. This new minister closed the service reminding us that it was Maundy Thursday, three days before Easter.

Nicholas associates a second event to his journey with me. A year later he came by for a visit and his hair and beard were darker. Nicholas explained that after two days of impeding my business, he said a prayer and asked God to make him less noticeable. God answered that prayer, granting Nicholas a changing of adornment. Each year beginning in mid-January his hair begins to darken, sometimes brown, sometimes black, occasionally blonde, and often Viking red. Nicholas is now able to wander among the people, visiting markets, attending Mass at different churches, helping in hospitals. Wherever he chooses to travel and wander, only those with unquestioned belief in the Magic of Christmas recognize him as Saint Nicholas. However, the incredible love in his heart keeps the sparkle glowing in his eyes, inviting people into his special magic. Then, as autumn fills the air, his hair and beard lighten until they are a soft white on December 6, the Feast of Saint Nicholas. But from December 24 through January 6, he is luminescent white, glowing from the inside and all who see him believe in the True Magic of the Christmas Season.

Nicholas surprised Kasandra in the summer of 1910 with an unexpected invitation to visit Alapuolella Pohjantähti (the North Pole). As if an after thought he added, "Oh, Jameson, you are welcome to join us . . . if you wish."

I had already made several visits to Nicholas' home and would never willingly miss an event such as this. It happened that we were in the village at the North Pole during midsummer. I was alarmed about midday, the day after Midsummer's Eve, when villagers started suddenly appearing. One by one, or in small groups, they just popped into view. When I asked one of the men what was happening I was referred to Liester, the librarian. It took me several hours to find this man of knowledge and would have missed him completely had I not been waiting in the library when he suddenly popped into view.

"Oh it is nothing too magical," the librarian laughed. "It is the Summer Solstice and many of us step into the second to catch up on work that needs to be finished."

I thought for a moment and remembered that Nicholas had told me about a solstice second on the Winter Solstice, but he said nothing about the Summer Solstice.

"Oh, yes," Liester explained. "It happens around the world two times each year, on the Winter Solstice and the Summer Solstice, the longest and shortest nights of the year. All you have to do is to clap your hands above your head, loudly mind you, at the instant the second occurs."

"How will I know when the second occurs?" I asked, filled with excitement.

"You just have to know. Some watch their clocks, others watch the stars. It normally occurs a few seconds past midnight, but you will know if you are meant to step into it."

"I have seen folks popping into view all day," I told the librarian. "How do you get out of the second?"

"Well, you will pop out normally when the second expires in twenty-four hours, or sixty days of second time. But if you need to step out early, you must return to where you were when you entered the second. Standing at that precise location, clap your hands over your head again."

There was a mysterious twinkle in Liester's eyes as he instructed me, but at the time I thought it was just his charm. Six months later I was working with Jakob, one of my distributors, helping him inventory his warehouse. We had already spent two days and accomplished very little as the man wanted to examine and re-price every piece. I wanted to be home by Christmas. When I overheard someone talking about the approaching Winter Solstice, I remembered the second. It was a crystal clear night so I stepped outside and after checking my watch, I looked at the stars. As an odd star approached the North Star, I raised my hands over my head.

It did not take long for me to appreciate how much energy a man can burn while moving boxes. All night long, actually several days for me, I moved boxes until I was completely exhausted. Shortly after sunrise, a work crew arrived to move the heavier crates so I figured I should step out of the second and rejoin the others. I went to the exact location where I had entered the second, just outside the doors of the warehouse, and there were three crates stacked where I needed to stand. I tried to move the crates, but they were extremely heavy.

Resigned to not waste time, I continued doing what I could without getting in the way. It was not long before I was too fatigued to continue and used what little energy I had left to step around the moving crates. They were moving slowly compared to myself, but I had to be alert lest I end up with a crate put on top of me. As I was about to pass out, I suffered an illusion that Nicholas was there and was slowly clapping his hands over his head. Still unable to get to my spot I decided to clap as Nicholas was demonstrating.

I awoke in a bed in Jakob's house with his wife pouring fruit juice down my throat. Nicholas was indeed standing there and asked me, "Why did you not step out when you got so tired?"

"Someone had put three heavy crates on my spot. They must have been filled with rocks because I was unable to move them," I explained, feeling much better after the juice.

"Your spot?" Nicholas asked. I could see by his face that he was very puzzled.

"The librarian told me I had to stand on the spot where I entered the second if I wanted to step out early," I explained.

Nicholas broke out into fits of laughter. When he could speak again, he told me, "Yes, Leister would tell you something like that. He is known for his pranks."

Kasandra and I were strolling home, hand in hand, from our daughter Inga's wedding. She was nineteen years old at the time and now married to a young man, Eric, who was already a very skilled mechanic. I believe he could fix almost any problem with a machine or mechanical device. It was near the end of summer and the perfect evening for a stroll, but I stray. As my wife and I came near our cottage I saw a familiar yet strange figure, or two of them actually. This figure was huge, its head almost reaching the line of my roof. I must admit also that I felt its features were almost grotesque. As we approached, it stood. Its head now reaching well above my roof line, I recognized our visitor, Orlf. Suddenly the grotesqueness was beautiful and I reached out to welcome the King of the Northern Norwegian Troll Kingdom, but was unable to move.

Kasandra was frozen and unyielding in her grip on my hand. The look on her face was not fear but unabated astonishment. I had told her about Orlf, however the reality of having him at our door was more than she could comprehend. Raising her hand, which held my hand in an iron tight grip, to my lips, I kissed her gently and then whispered, "I need to greet our guest." She slowly turned her head toward me and began to breathe again, relaxing her grip on my hand. Again I stepped forward, this time successfully, with my hand extended.

After a very polite bow and unusual handshake, Orlf stood quietly and waited. Staring at the large troll, I remembered our last meeting.

"Orlf, I would like you to meet my wife of twenty-three years and six months. Kasandra, this is Orlf.

"Orlf, I am pleased to tell you that we are returning from the wedding of our second daughter, Inga. She is now married to Eric, a young man who works on machines. Our oldest daughter, Kristina, is also married, for two years now. She and her husband, Jorge, have just had a daughter whom they named Hannah after my wife's mother. Our son, Artur, is now fifteen years old and helps me when I do the work of Nicholas, but he is not interested in my regular work with art." I then stood as still as I could and waited.

After just one minute, Orlf smiled and replied, "I am good to meet you, Kasandra, wife of the friend of Nicholas. I like that you came from your Inga's wedding. My wife, Orchrhred, and I have a daughter since we talked. We have ten children, but two sons are killed by the cold. Our village has plenty deer and should have a safe cold this."

Orlf then got very quiet and waited. Not knowing what to do I asked, "Orlf, friend of Nicholas, you have someone with you. Do you need my help?"

"Lundar," Orlf announced proudly, "my seventh son travels on my back with me. He is hurt in a man trap and want . . . need help."

"Yes, I will see Lundar, but my wife, Kasandra, needs to go inside. Will you please move off the door?" I waved my hand slightly to indicate Orlf should move to the left a step or two making it possible for Kasandra to get by. As she reached for the door I asked, "Maybe some oat cakes?"

Kasandra smiled and slipped inside briefly. While I was looking at Lundar's leg, she returned with two sacks of oat cakes. She handed both to Orlf who took a piece out of one of the sacks and smiled broadly. He then handed the other sack to Lundar announcing, "GOOD."

Lundar appeared to be a smaller version of his father. At the age of twenty-three he was still very young for a troll, similar in maturity to my son Artur, who was fifteen years old. As I looked at the young troll, I immediately saw he was missing his left leg, from just below the knee. The injury had healed over and showed no signs of decay or infection. I was about to question Orlf as to what he wanted me to do for Lundar when my father-in-law, mother-in-law, and son arrived.

"Splendid wedding . . ." Lars called out before he realized I had company. Stopping about six meters from the house he grabbed Hannah and Artur and tried desperately to analyze the situation.

Stepping forward, I diffused a potentially explosive scene. "Orlf, Friend of Nicholas and King of the Northern Norwegian Troll Kingdom, I would like to introduce to you my son, Artur." I signaled Artur to step forward and wait while I continued. "This is Lars, the father of my wife, Kasandra, and with him is his wife, Hannah, the mother of my wife, Kasandra." I then signaled Lars and Hannah to step forward.

Artur showed no hesitancy and was very delighted to meet not just a troll, but a KING as well. Lars and Hannah were very slow to step forward and I fear they almost insulted the king with their delay. Orlf was a gentleman, as he had been all evening, and greeted Lars and Hannah warmly.

"And WHAT or who is this?" Lars asked gruffly and pointing at Lundar.

"Lars, it is very fortunate you arrived when you did," I began to explain. "This is Lundar, the seventh son of Orlf, and he has a problem I believe you can solve." I helped Lundar to stand and quickly learned that while he was a smaller version of his father, he was much larger than myself. "You see, Lundar has lost his lower left leg to a man trap. Looking at the rest of this young troll I imagine he is having quite the problem running with other young trolls."

Orlf smiled at my understanding and nodded approvingly.

"The boy needs a peg-leg, just like an old seaman," Lars replied without hesitation.

"How long will it take you to fashion a new leg for this young troll?" I asked with as much enthusiasm as I could muster.

"Hannah can fashion a sleeve to fit over the leg and I

should be able to turn the base and leg in a day or so."

"Can you fashion the leg so it will be strong enough to hold this growing young troll as he lumbers through the forest?" I asked, trying to insure that Lars had considered the weight that would be on the peg-leg.

"You are right, less turning, sturdier stock. I can have it finished by this time tomorrow. Where will I find our friend when I am ready? Is he staying with you?"

"Orlf, Lars, the father of my wife, Kasandra, has agreed to help repair your son. He needs to work for one day. Where do you wish to sleep this night and wait until the sun begins to sleep tomorrow?"

"Your people would not like to see Orlf and Lundar at your home. We sleep with trees and come back with next sun." He then presented me with two empty sacks and waited. I understood the hint and stepped inside to refill the sacks with oat cakes. Kasandra was beside herself with worry, but I assured her everything would be all right. We had only enough oat cakes to half-fill both sacks, still Orlf smiled when I presented them to him. He then lifted his son over his shoulder, without a word, and stomped across the road into the forest beyond.

When they had disappeared, I invited Lars and Hannah inside. "Thank you for your offer to help; both of you. Can you really make a leg for Lundar in just a day?"

"I doubt it," Hannah laughed. "He forgot to get measurements."

"I do not need measurements of the troll," Lars replied indignantly. "I shall never forget the sight of seeing Jameson, father of my grandchildren, holding up that young . . . young troll. His leg was cut off five inches below your knee and was twice as big around plus another half."

"Be sure to make the sleeve a bit large for growing room," I chuckled.

After a brief visit and a glass of wine to toast the events of the day, Lars and Hannah went home to begin work on Lundar's leg.

"I need some wax polish," Lars announced at his arrival,

about mid-afternoon the next day.

I pushed a can of polish toward him and he quickly went to work polishing a beautifully turned oak post. It was as big around as my leg, my upper leg, and was truly a work of art. The sleeve was heavy sail canvas and was finished with two leather belts. I looked inside, where the leg stump would rest, and found a hefty pad that should never wear out. Well, maybe not for five or six years, anyway.

Lars was just putting the last bit of polish on the post when Artur rushed into my shop. "They are back!"

We all went outside and greeted Orlf and Lundar. Lars began by rushing up to Lundar with the new leg, but I grabbed him and held him back until all the pleasantries were finished. It took ten minutes to say "Hello" and find how they had spent the night and the day. When both Orlf and Lundar stood quietly, I stepped forward and propped Lundar up while Lars fitted the new leg over the Lundar's stump. It fit well, just a bit of growing room. One of the leather belts buckled below the knee, on the stump, and the other above the knee. The sleeve was open in the front to allow flexing of the knee itself.

Lundar stepped on it several times, discovering it to be a smidge too long, then leapt into air landing squarely on both legs at the same time. The young troll's eyes grew wide and he smiled at Artur. Before I could stop either of them, they were running down the road.

Ten minutes later they came running back and Artur fell on the ground laughing so hard he could not breathe. Lundar stood proudly next to his father. When Artur caught his breath, he told us, "Thom Johansson. He was about to kiss Inger Brigman when Lundar and I came racing past them. I think Inger had her eyes closed, but Thom . . . Thom will never be the same again!"

I took custodial possession of The Woodsman's staff in December 1890, just over thirty years ago. Working with Nicholas has taught me more about working with people and learning how to help them than studies at any university could have. With this unusual man at my side, my family has survived tough economic times and celebrated amazing triumphs. I have met artists of incredible talent and developed strong friendships with two wonderful distributors.

Adam Smythe, the Englishman in northern Norway, has shown a true talent for being completely unpredictable. He took his nephew with him to meet Gunther Roland, the man who carves ships from logs. While through my one encounter I thought the nephew was without personality, the artist's daughter found him to be intriguing. Florence and Oscar were married and built a house three hundred meters from Gunther, just the right distance for the grandfather of five. When visiting Gunther I find him just returning from, just going to, or at his daughter's home playing with grandchildren, but he has never run out of ships. Adam, on the other hand, could never make up his mind about what he wanted in his shop. He often turns down pieces I had acquired just for him in favor of ordinary troll work (some actually done by trolls) and other days nothing satisfies him. Visits with Adam are both challenging and delightful.

Karl Nielsen died at the comfortable age of eighty-two. I was told he kissed his wonderful wife good night and went to sleep. He must have had wonderful dreams for he was smiling, but then I never saw him when he was not filled with joy. I have continued to work with his family, who took over his business, and enjoy every visit.

My other two distributors, Gunther and Jakob, continued to purchase small numbers of pieces until they each retired, about five years apart. Gunther simply closed his door one day, however Jakob sold his business and I continue to work with the young man who purchased it. We have learned a lot about art from each other - he is a university graduate and really knows little about art or business, but he knows how to make people happy, which I guess is the basis for any successful business.

Roy Brok, my neighbor who wrestles with branches, became a very well known artist but has never learned to tell time. His children grew up one day while he was working on a masterpiece and he found grandchildren running around when he finished. If it were not for his wife, Rebecca, the man would starve to death with a full larder and fresh bread at his elbow.

Orlf and Lundar come by the shop from to time. Several of the trolls learned to carve trees into unusual art forms, which sell very well. Lundar enjoys visiting while delivering the current inventory of works. On their last visit I noticed that Lundar was as tall as his father yet had never asked for a longer leg. I looked down and saw that he had nailed several flat planks to the bottom of the original leg my father-in-law had prepared for him. As he grew, he simply extended the length of the leg with planks.

Kasandra and I have lived a wonderful life, in part thanks to my relationship with Nicholas. We have five grandchildren: three from Kristina and two so far from Inga, but Artur has given me the greatest heartbreak and joy of all. Artur has never enjoyed the art business and has looked for a new and different purpose to his life. He has helped me assist other families, with and without the direction of Nicholas, but last week he came to me and said, "Far, I am going to America."

"What? What do you mean?" I fumbled to understand.

"America is having difficult times and they need the services of *The Woodsman*."

"America is a big country, and far away. How do you plan to get there and where will you begin?" I asked with growing concern.

"I have saved money I earned working around the village, and I can work onboard ship during the crossing. As for where to begin? If you see a hundred people in need of help, which do you choose to help first?"

"I suppose you help the first person you come to," I replied with a growing smile.

"Then that is what I shall do. I will ask Nicholas who needs my help the most and go there."

"Have you told your mother?"

"No. . . . I will let you do that."

I rolled my eyes and took a deep breath. "Kasandra, can you come here for just a moment, please?"

My beautiful wife joined our conversation, wiping her hands on a towel. "Yes?"

"Artur tells me he wants to be *The Woodsman* in America."

"Yes?" she smiled broadly, without surprise as she tucked the towel into her apron. "So when will you be leaving?"

"If you can fix me some bread and cheese and smoked meat tomorrow, I will leave the next day," Artur chuckled.

"I can have it ready for you tonight if you wish."

"No, I want to visit my sisters before I go and say good-bye to some friends."

"Okay, dinner will be ready in a few moments." Kasandra then kissed Artur on the cheek, kissed me on my forehead, and returned to preparing dinner for the three of us.

Throughout the next day I tried to think of what advice I needed to give my son as he embarked on such a grande adventure, but I could not think of a thing. I had given him twenty-one years of advice, teaching, instruction, and lessons; now he was stepping into the world to use his life's knowledge. We were just finishing our last dinner together when there was a knock at the door. Artur got up to answer the knock.

"I heard a rumor on the wind that a new *Woodsman* was about to embark on a tremendous adventure," Nicholas said with a joyful voice.

While Artur grabbed his bag, Nicholas joined Kasandra and me at the table, nibbling on the cake made for Artur. Moments barely passed before an eager young man stood before us, ready to launch himself into the world. I realized at that instant that there was one gift I had to give my son. As Nicholas and Artur walked toward the door I went into my office and retrieved a small box, which I had acquired some months before. Stopping at the door I retrieved *The Woodsman's Staff*. Staring at the head of this magnificent symbol of my relationship with Nicholas, I felt incredibly honored.

"Artur, if you are going to be *The Woodsman* perhaps you should carry *The Staff*. I am confident you will make good use of it." Beaming with anticipation, my son took *The Woodsman's Staff*.

"One other gift. I was going to save this for your birthday, but I suppose it is time." I handed my son the box I had retrieved from my office. "Nicholas can explain its significance better than I but I hope it will remind you that your mother and I are here, anytime you need to restore your balance."

Artur opened the box and found a golden pocket watch. An image of a reindeer was embossed on the top. After winding it a few turns, he opened it, finding the words "Share Your Life" engraved on the inside cover. Turning the watch over, he pressed the top knob once more and the back opened. Inside he saw the gears turning in perfect balance. "I know the story Far. You have told me many times using your own watch."

Dropping the watch in his pocket, he gave his mother and me a final hug, then stepped into Nicholas' sleigh. As the old man whistled to his team, I noticed that there were four reindeer in the harness; I had always seen only two. Before the whistle faded, the sleigh and my son had disappeared.

Other books by author E Gale Buck

The lineage of Santa's Woodsmen ...

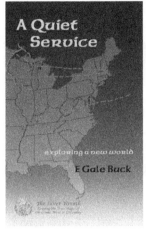

exploring a new world Arthur Thorpe was the fifth in this unusual lineage. His story begins in Norway, son of the fourth *Woodsman*. As a young man he read about problems in America, following the first world war. Believing he could make a difference, he came to the United States of America. This journal chronicles not only his efforts to help a weary land but also his hunger to explore the vast reaches of a remarkable country. During an age when selfless service was sorely needed, yet not easily found, Arthur found adventure, romance, heartache, and opportunity beyond his expectations.

passion beyond misfortune In 1932 Maxwell Kartar, the sixth Woodsman of Saint Nicholas, served only one day, yet his wife, Edith, continued to serve on her own as the seventh in this proud lineage. Merging Max's passions into her own and later adopting those of Nicholas, she became a formidable force within her community. Jimmy Norfleet, the eighth Woodsman, lost his wife at an early age, yet their passion took root within their daughter. Bethany succeeded her father, becoming Nicholas' ninth partner in service to Christmas. Filled with troubles and successes, love and loss, sunshine and rain, their stories are uncommon. Their passion for each day helped them rise above misfortunes, lifting others as well.

A Quiet Service - *reaching beyond tomorrow* Jonathon Syzmoor was the first, in 1831. His legacy of working with Saint Nicholas continues to this day around the world. Men and women have answered the call from Nicholas to do more and expect nothing in return, to share their lives without expectation. Each of these servants has a story. *Reaching beyond tomorrow* contains the stories of the four most recent members of this lineage, reaching from 1972 to today and beyond tomorrow. These final chapters of the lineage of Santa's Woodsmen also include Natasaha's ("Mrs. Claus") story, and Alapouella Pohjantähti ("The North Pole"). Scheduled for release November 2020.

Other books about Santa's Woodsmen...

Jonathon Syzmoor, orphaned at the age of eleven in early 1800s Scandinavia, left his home to get an education. Returning home six years later he made an uncommon contract with the richest man in town. After one year Jonathon held the seat of power and married his soul-mate. Tragedy struck again and Jonathon immersed himself in business. Awakened from his soulless world by the generosity of his grandson Jonathon made another agreement, this time with a man in a long red cape. This agreement changed his life and has effected the lives of countless others ever since.

When Gale Buck became the 13th in the Lineage of Santa's Woodsmen, in October 2007, Nicholas agreed that his task should be to help others find the True Magic of Christmas in Everyday. Nicholas made the letters, journals, logs and personal notes of the previous eleven Woodsmen available to Gale. While assembling the 'Secrets of Santa revealed by his Woodsmen,[1] a new story unfolded, the story of Nicholas. Through these stories told by his Woodsmen, the man behind the legend of Santa Claus, Saint Nicholas, is revealed as never before.

Many Santa friends wanted the "Secrets of Santa" so they could tell them as stories on visits with children blessed with belief, and maybe a few older children who still wish to believe. So for the Santas, parents, babysitters, and other storytellers who wish to share the Magic of Christmas, we offer this collection of secrets from "Finding Nicholas - the secrets of santa revealed by his woodsmen." Each story includes hints on how to make it your own.

More Stories from The North Pole

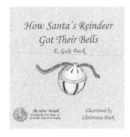

All books available through www.amazon.com

Please visit www.santaswoodsman.com for more information

A Quiet Service   *a scandinavian legacy*

CPSIA information can be obtained
at www.ICGtesting.com
Printed in the USA
LVHW091815280420
654553LV00002B/158